Jimmy Evans and the New School

This above all: to thine own self be true,
And it must follow, as the night the day,
Thou canst not then be false to any man.

Hamlet, I.iii 81-3

Geoff Stock

O&U
Onwards & Upwards

Onwards and Upwards Publishers

4 The Old Smithy, London Road, Rockbeare,
EX5 2EA, United Kingdom.
www.onwardsandupwards.org

First edition, published in the United Kingdom by Onwards and Upwards Publishers Ltd. (2022).

ISBN: 978-1-78815-889-3
Typeface: Sabon LT
Illustrator: Hannah Stout

This is a work of fiction. Names, characters, businesses, places, events, locales, and incidents are either the products of the author's imagination or used in a fictitious manner. Any resemblance to actual persons, living or dead, or actual events is purely coincidental.

Author's acknowledgements:

My sincere thanks to Luke, Anna, Pete, Geraldine, Jo, Vera, Freddie, David and so many supportive friends.

And, above all, my Author.

CONTENTS

1

THE SHOP WINDOW

Jimmy looked longingly in through the shop window.

"If only…" he thought.

His eyes had focussed on the bright orange pair of boys' football boots that were displayed in the absolute centre of the shop window at head height to Jimmy.

He knew he would never be the proud owner of those boots. Mum and Dad could never afford to buy him a pair like that. They would be way too pricey, he was sure. The very fact that the price tag was not showing told him that – and the fact that they were the most prominent pair in the window.

And of course the boots themselves. They were perfect. And the right size too, Jimmy knew. Just by looking at them he could tell. Okay, so he would try them on, of course. But what was the point? He was never gonna have them. So that was it. *Come on, Jimmy!* he told himself. *Best get home. Mum will be wondering.*

He turned away from the shop window, and as he did, he noticed a familiar figure across the road, looking in his direction. Uncle Reg. He was using his mobile phone.

"Hi, Uncle Reg!" called Jimmy.

"Hi Jimmy – you OK? Can't talk now. But see you soon."

A dejected Jimmy made his way back home. "Someone will be lucky enough one day to own those boots," he said to himself ruefully. "But no way will that be me."

2

TIME TO DECIDE

"Good day at school, Jimmy?" Mum asked, as he came in through the door.

"Hmm – OK," he replied, not sure what else to say. The only really good things to have happened were lunch- and breaktimes. Which was pretty much the same most days. Lunch today had been one of his favourites: quiche, salad and chips. Delicious. Then of course during break he played 'footy' with his mates. That was always good. But nothing good ever happened in class. Well, *hardly* ever.

"I've had a letter asking us to state our choices for your new school," Mum announced. "Eastgate is nice and close. Shall we put that one down?"

Jimmy thought for a moment. Eastgate School was nearby, yes, and so it would be easy for travel. But his best mates Brendan and Luke were keen to go to Graysfield, because they lived closer to that school.

There was another consideration too. And to Jimmy it was all-important. Graysfield had a football team. That was rare. Most of the schools in the area did not.

"How about Graysfield?" Jimmy suggested. "I'd like to go there."

"Well, I don't know what your chances would be," answered Mum. "We don't exactly live close to Graysfield. So if you did go there you'd need to leave very early to catch the bus."

Jimmy thought that would be a fair price to pay for going to a school with his mates – and football. True, he may not get into the team. But he'd give it a go. And even if he didn't make the team, there would be the practices.

"I'd still like to go to Graysfield," he insisted.

Yes, Jimmy was desperately keen to get into any school which had a football club. He wasn't brilliant – he would be the first to admit that. But it was his favourite sport – he certainly enjoyed the football at his present school – and he simply loved scoring goals!

So Mum, keen for Jimmy to be happy at his new school, put Graysfield as first choice, with Eastgate second. Now it was just a case of 'hang on and hope'…

3

BIRTHDAY BOY

It was the morning of Jimmy's eleventh birthday. His alarm woke him, but not fully. For a moment he was halfway between his dream and his bedroom. Then, as he rubbed his eyes, he remembered what day it was...

"Whoa, yes!" he exclaimed. "My birthday! *Yippee!*" He gave himself a good stretch before bouncing out of bed and hurrying to the bathroom.

As it was his birthday, Jimmy wanted to look his best – so he made sure he cleaned his teeth, washed his face and his clothes were smart. But he was trying to do it all at a hundred miles an hour, which meant toothpaste was landing on the washbasin mirror and soap on the floor; this left him with a fair amount of cleaning up to do, taking up valuable birthday time. Nevertheless, he hurtled downstairs in high spirits and helped himself to a bowl of cereal in the kitchen, where Mum was busy at the sink.

"Happy birthday, Jimmy!" she called, drying her hands. "Have a good day at school."

"Thanks, Mum!" replied Jimmy, pouring himself a glass of orange juice.

He gulped it down and was just about to pour a second glass when – *clatter, clatter!* – the post arrived through the letterbox.

Jimmy ran out to the front door. He scooped up the morning's impressive postal delivery and hurried back into the kitchen to enjoy his pile.

One by one, the envelopes were opened and checked out. Apart from all the cards, he had been given a good amount of money, some of which he knew those giving could barely afford. He felt thankful.

Then he noticed an envelope larger than the others, and with a typed address. Looking closer, he realised it was addressed to "Mrs. J. Evans". He handed it over to his mum.

On seeing the envelope, she gave out an involuntary "Oh!" which she then tried to turn into a throat-clearing sound – unsuccessfully! Unfortunately for Mum, it was exactly the sort of combination of sounds that would be likely to make Jimmy just a little suspicious.

"What is it, Mum?" he asked, curious to know.

She opened the letter. It was a communication from the Education Department of the City Council, and was headed:

School Allocation

Jimmy's Mum had not expected the reply to arrive so soon, and she was anxious lest it should contain disappointing news, especially on Jimmy's birthday. *Oh, please, please may he have been allocated Graysfield!* she prayed silently.

"I just need to go and read this letter a moment," Mum said. "I'll be back soon." And with that, she poured Jimmy another glass of orange and slipped out into the front room.

———————————

Mum returned to the kitchen just as Jimmy was polishing off his toast and marmalade. She went over to the kitchen unit and picked up a rather large envelope, which Jimmy noticed had something in it, and she added the letter she had just read.

"Here's another card, Jimmy," smiled Mum, popping it on to the table in front of him.

He quickly opened the envelope, to find a large birthday card with blue-and-white-shirted footballers pictured playing on the front. Opening it, he saw it was from Mum and Dad, and he was delighted to also find a crisp ten pound note there along with a simple message:

Happy Birthday, Jimmy.
Love from Mum and Dad.

"Ah, thanks, Mum!" he beamed.

Jimmy and his mum were very close. He was an only child, and his dad worked from dawn till dusk in a newsagent's shop he had started from scratch five years ago. Though it was hard, tiring work, and did nothing for his health, his dad had chosen it that way. He had in that time built up a very good customer base and was well respected in the area. But it was no way to make a fortune. Every penny was hard earned, and there was never much to spare. It also meant, on most days, Jimmy saw little of his dad until early evening. Except, that was, for a few days a year when Uncle Reg took over the shop, to enable the family to have a short, well-earned break together.

"Now, don't forget to read the letter too," advised Mum.

Jimmy carefully took out the letter his mother had added to the envelope. "It's addressed to you, Mum."

"I'd like *you* to read it, Jimmy," she replied.

Jimmy was not a particularly good reader, but as soon as he saw the heading he concentrated hard on the words to find out what the letter had to say. For a moment he was tense, unsure where the letter was leading. But by the end it was perfectly clear. It read:

Dear Mrs. Evans,

Thank you for your completed application regarding your son Jimmy's Secondary School. I have to tell you that your residence lies well within the catchment area of Eastgate School, and so Jimmy would normally be expected to attend that school.

However, we note your preference for Graysfield School and, after full checks and consultation with the Graysfield headmaster, we are satisfied that his school does in fact have capacity such as will allow Jimmy to attend there.

Unless I hear otherwise from you within seven days, I shall assume you are accepting a place for Jimmy at Graysfield.

With kind regards,

J D Knapp

J. D. Knapp, B.C.C.
Education Committee Secretary

So, he had been offered a place at Graysfield School, just as he had hoped.

"YES-S-S!" he exclaimed, jumping up and punching the air. He went over to Mum and gave her a hug. "Wow! This is the best birthday present I could possibly have had," he declared. "It's a great start to the day!"

"It certainly is, Jimmy," agreed Mum. "Now, you had better fetch your bag and get ready for school."

Jimmy fetched his bag, said goodbye to his mum and hurried out of the house.

"Looks like a really *good* day!" he said to himself as he hurried down the road. "Can't wait to tell Brendan and Luke!"

Even at school, things continued to go unusually well for Jimmy. As he walked up to the school gate, he saw his two special mates, Brendan and Luke, there waiting for him.

"Happy birthday, Jimmy!" they chorused. The boys knew Jimmy's parents could not afford to invite his friends round for a party. They were okay with that – they understood. And so they had each bought him a little gift, hand-wrapped, with a card.

"Ah, my favourite!" cried Jimmy, swiftly unwrapping a Chocolate Orange given him by Luke.

"Bet you won't guess what I've got you!" teased Brendan, whose packet did at least have some Sellotape on it.

"Nope – I can't!" agreed Jimmy, wondering. Fascinated, he attacked the Sellotape. The paper came off – and yes, Jimmy *was* surprised.

"A box of paints," he said, "and some brushes. Wow, thanks, Bren!"

"I wasn't sure what I'd get you," admitted Brendan, frankly, "so I went to Bargain World. They were only a pound. And the brushes were half-price at 50p."

Brendan, as you can tell, was a frank and honest boy, though he sometimes lacked tact.

Jimmy was no artist. In fact, there were few things he was good at, really. Even at football he had to try very hard to achieve anything. But he was a boy who appreciated kindness. He thanked Brendan again, popped his presents into his school bag, then the three lads, hearing the bell, moved on towards the classroom.

Even the school day was better than expected. Jimmy scored his highest ever mark in the class spelling test in first lesson, with nine out of twenty. Considering his average was five or six, and he had scored several zeroes, he was really pleased. As was his teacher. And she awarded him a credit for progress!

In maths lesson, too, Jimmy found the courage to raise his hand to answer several questions. His answers were all wrong, but nevertheless the teacher gave him another credit for interest and effort.

Lunch was one of his favourites – really tasty fish, chips and peas, with a chocolate mousse to follow. Then in breaktime he enjoyed a great game of 'footy' with his mates, scoring twice and laying on three other goals.

The school day finished with dodgeball in P.E., again loved by all the class. Jimmy was doing well until he ran into the rolling ball. But he didn't mind. It had been a great game – and for once, a really good school day.

Today Jimmy decided he would walk home via the sports shop. He just wanted to check that the orange boots were still there in pride of place in the shop window. Most likely he could never afford them, but then you never knew. If he could top up his birthday money with a little more in the next few weeks for helping Mum in the house, then maybe he might come closer to the price of the boots, in time for his arrival at Graysfield.

He turned the corner approaching the shop. They really were the best, the smartest boots he had ever seen. It would be so good just to see them there, in all their glory in the shop window.

He arrived at the shop. He looked in through the window. Then he blinked and looked again. *The boots were not there.* Everything else appeared exactly as before. But the boots had disappeared.

4

MOVING ON

As Jimmy walked through the door of his house, he really wanted to share with Mum all the great things that had happened at school that day: the presents from Luke and Bren; the credits in both English and maths; the delicious lunch; the 'footy' and goals in breaktime; and the fun in dodgeball. But somehow the sight of the sports shop window without the boots remained clearly in his mind, clouding over everything else.

"Good day at school, Jimmy?" asked Mum.

Jimmy hesitated.

Mum could see he was not happy, but knew he would tell her in his own way.

Just then the doorbell rang. Mum went to the door. It was Uncle Reg.

"Just popping in with something for the birthday boy," he announced. "Can't stop – I'm wanted at home."

Jimmy, hearing his uncle's voice, rushed to the door.

"Happy birthday, Jimmy!" greeted Uncle Reg, handing him a brightly wrapped parcel.

"Oh, thank you, Uncle Reg!" replied Jimmy, taking the parcel. He couldn't wait to see what was inside. He tore off the wrapping paper to reveal a rectangular cardboard box.

Jimmy lifted the lid of the box and gasped in amazement and sheer delight. Inside the box, amid large amounts of crumpled tissue paper was a superb pair of orange football

"Oh, thank you, Uncle Reg!" replied Jimmy,
taking the parcel.

boots – instantly recognised by Jimmy as the ones he had longed for in the sports shop window.

"Oh, Uncle Reg, these are just what I wanted. But however did you know?"

"I saw you looking at them in the shop window," replied Reg. "When I saw how your eyes were fixed on the boots, I phoned the store and asked them to make sure they put them aside until I could go in and purchase them."

Jimmy then remembered seeing Uncle Reg using his phone as he had turned away from the shop.

"Uncle Reg, you have completed my perfect day!" beamed Jimmy.

"You're welcome, Jimmy," he replied, smiling, "and I hope they bring you great fun and enjoyment."

Jimmy couldn't wait to try out his new boots at the school football club. This was usually held after school on Thursday, and sure enough, Jimmy went along with his boots on the next possible occasion.

The great thing about the boots was, not only did they fit perfectly, they seemed to give his toes and feet the space to perform in a way which made Jimmy feel a far better player than before. He had a great practice that Thursday, scoring four goals and laying on another for the ever-alert Taha. *Yes, they were great boots.*

Sadly there were no more practices that season at his old school, bad weather bringing an early end to proceedings. So Jimmy, not really into summer sports, set his mind on making a real go of it when he would move on to Graysfield.

That summer, the family were given a surprise treat. Uncle Reg offered to look after the shop, not just for a few days but for a whole fortnight, so that the family could have a well-earned break. Jimmy was thrilled, as it was his final holiday before starting at Graysfield. Uncle Reg owned a holiday apartment in Cornwall, and often let it out to his workmates and their families, who would pay to have a delightful seaside holiday. Uncle Reg now refused to accept any payment. "Just take sufficient spending money, and the apartment is yours," he said to Dad. "I'll take care of the shop, and if you want to give me something, when you return we'll all go out for a meal and you can buy me a drink." Uncle Reg was like that – generous to the core. And nothing Dad (or Mum) said would have swayed him.

It was a wonderful holiday. Mum said she couldn't remember a time when Dad had been so relaxed, as the whole family had a whale of a time down by the sea. The weather was near perfect, and everyone splashed around in the sea most days, before spoiling themselves in one of the town's many seaside restaurants.

But all too soon came the end of the holidays and return to school.

At least it's Graysfield, mused Jimmy. *I'll have Bren and Luke there – and, of course, 'footy'.*

The three boys had arranged to meet at the school gates before school on the first day, and to go in together. Graysfield was a smart, modern school with well-designed classrooms, plenty of labs and IT facilities, and an abundance of green 'leisure areas'. Jimmy was secretly impressed, though also dreading the lessons.

The first morning was spent largely in issuing books, timetables and instructions. There was also, however, a 'large assembly', when the whole of his year was addressed by the head of year and the pastoral head. Jimmy quite liked this session; it sounded as though this big school really did care about its pupils, and Jimmy began to believe he might stand a chance of getting something out of his experience here.

So it was a positive Jimmy who returned home on the first day of his new term at Graysfield. Mum was relieved. It was a big issue, moving to secondary school, and the first day was important.

"Just do your best, and that's all I can ask," his mum had said many times. And Jimmy, knowing how hard his dad worked in the shop and his mum in the house looking after him, was an honest trier.

But he was no high flier. He struggled with all of the core subjects: English, maths and science. And he had little interest in any of the others either, except for P.E. He wasn't even particularly good at that, but he did love games and anything where he could run around and express himself. Everything else was more of an endurance test, really.

First lesson after lunch on the second day was history. The teacher was Mr. Kenny. But there was something about Mr. Kenny which straight away appealed to Jimmy. He was fun. And as he was fun, so was what he taught. Listening to Mr. Kenny, Jimmy actually imagined he was a deckhand on board the 'Golden Hind' as it sailed across the oceans under Sir Francis Drake. Yes, history could be a fun subject.

So as the first week wore on, Jimmy began to feel more at home in Graysfield. And lists were starting to go up on noticeboards announcing after-school activities.

On Wednesday morning, football club was announced, and Jimmy promptly put his name down on the list. As did Luke and Bren.

Practices would be held after school on Tuesdays, beginning the following week. Jimmy was hoping the days would not drag too much before the first practice would come around. A few more exciting lessons like Mr. Kenny's history would certainly help.

5

THE OLD LADY ON THE BUS

Jimmy soon found that setting his alarm for seven o'clock instead of seven-thirty was not that bad after all. It gave him time to have his breakfast and gather his bags before leaving to catch the seven-forty bus at the end of the road.

He enjoyed the bus rides too. They took him through parts of the town he and not visited before, and it was interesting to see shops and offices opening up and people beginning their daily routines as he travelled to school. But it was a journey home which he was to remember later for a rather different reason.

It was market day, and the bus was fuller than usual when Jimmy stepped on after school that evening. Gradually the bus become fuller and fuller, and by now all seats on the lower deck where Jimmy was seated were occupied. Several young men and a couple of teenage girls got on at Market Square and went straight for the upper deck. Then Jimmy noticed an old lady getting on. She seemed to have several bags full of shopping, and was struggling to present her bus pass. As she eventually moved on to the lower deck, Jimmy realised that all the seats were taken. Instinctively, he got up and offered her his seat.

"Thank you so much," she responded graciously, as she worked her way on to the seat.

Jimmy was glad he had offered up his seat. He always felt a trifle embarrassed standing up for a person he didn't know, but this lady was around the same age as his own gran; he hoped someone would have done the same for her. There was no way he could feel comfortable seeing an old lady like that standing with all her shopping.

Several stops later, there was a mass exodus. It was Bentley Crossroads. Everyone got off here – well, *most* people. It was a big shopping hub, but also had many residential roads nearby. There were plenty of seats available now. Jimmy was about to hop into one when he heard a voice. It was the old lady.

"Would you like to sit here? There's a space now."

Sure enough, there were spare seats now around the old lady. Maybe she was lonely or just wanted a chat. Jimmy sat down on the seat across the aisle from her.

"I see from your uniform that you attend Graysfield School," said the old lady. "I know it well. In fact, my grandson went to school there."

Jimmy replied politely, "Oh, that's interesting," but couldn't think of anything else to say.

Fortunately, the old lady helped him out. "Yes, he always wanted to go to Graysfield – and do you know why?"

Before Jimmy could work out a sensible reply, the old lady broke in again.

"Football, it was!" she said. "Yes, he was football crazy. That's why he wanted to go there."

Jimmy's face – his whole being – lit up. He had lost his shyness when he replied, "Amazing! That's exactly why I chose Graysfield. Yes – I love football, too, and that's what helps me to like Graysfield as a school."

By now Jimmy was just two stops away from where he needed to get off the bus.

"What I always loved," said the old lady, "was going along to support their special occasions – you know, fairs, concerts, sports days. They had some really nice teachers, and everyone was so pleasant."

Jimmy assured the old lady that Graysfield still did have plenty of special events and occasions, some of which visitors could apply online to attend.

"I'll be looking out then," replied the old lady. "My life is pretty lonely these days – I miss the company I used to have."

As Jimmy said goodbye and left the bus, he wondered whether he could help the old lady get in touch with Graysfield about events.

As usual, Mum had an answer. "If you see her again, you can hand her one of these," she said, handing him a Graysfield calendar handbook. "For some reason they've sent me two."

Jimmy carefully put the calendar inside his blazer pocket before hanging up the blazer and changing into his T-shirt.

———————————

Sure enough, two days later the old lady had again been shopping, this time for birthday presents, when Jimmy spotted her boarding the bus. He waited for her to be seated before starting a chat and handing her the Graysfield calendar which Mum had given him for her.

"I shall certainly try to come along before long. Thank you," the old lady said gratefully.

"You're welcome," he replied. "By the way, my name is Jimmy. I told Mum about you, and she has put our address on the calendar, in case you would like to pop in for a cup of tea and a chat anytime."

"Oh, how lovely," replied the old lady. "My name is Mary. Mary Treasure. I live on Norton Street, close to the Broadley Walk Medical Centre."

The bus had arrived at Jimmy's stop. He smiled at the old lady and they wished each other well as he left the bus, eager to share the latest news with his mum.

6

NOT QUITE TO PLAN

At last it was Tuesday afternoon, and Jimmy's class were nearing the end of a gruelling maths lesson. Geometry had been the order of the day, and Jimmy had not been able to draw a circle for toffee. His compass work was not good. He had tried and tried, without success.

The bell brought double relief. He could cease his labours in the world of circles. And it was time for football club – his first ever at Graysfield. How good was that!

Class was dismissed, and Jimmy hurried with Luke and Brendan to the changing rooms. Everyone was excited and eager to get down to the playing field for the football practice. Jimmy, Brendan and Luke went down together. They soon reached the pitch, where they saw Mr. Smith (or 'Smithy', as the boys called him), ready with notebook and pencil. Smithy was the head of games, and also the coach for the Graysfield football team.

As they arrived, they were told to put on their boots and run around the pitch. Several boys were already running; others were tying up their boots, while some were just arriving. As Jimmy put on his special orange boots, he felt a warm glow of delight. They were more than comfortable. They felt perfect.

Smithy had set out lines of plastic cones in such a way that those who had completed a circuit of the pitch could fetch a ball and dribble in and out of a line of cones before passing the ball to another and completing a shorter jog. That done, they would then go to the coach.

As the stragglers were catching up, he addressed the boys: "Welcome to Graysfield football! I have three rules, three wishes: *listen, learn, enjoy*. That's it. Any questions?"

There were none. I mean, anyone as clear and decisive as that was surely not one to be trifled with, so it was clearly not the time for unnecessary comments. The boys waited for the coach to continue.

"I have one thing to add at this stage, boys," he said. "I'm delighted to say, we have a match arranged for next Wednesday at St. Mary's School. So... play well today and you could be in the team!"

The boys buzzed with excitement.

"One further question before we start. Have any of you had experience playing in goal?"

Four boys tentatively raised a hand.

"You two can play in goal in the first half," Smithy said, calling out two of the boys to stand either side of him. "You others will take your turn in the second half."

The coach had ensured that a maximum of twenty-two players would attend the practice, and sure enough, precisely twenty-two boys had appeared, making it easy for him to select two teams. Within the next minute, he had placed in each team four defenders, four midfield players and two strikers.

"Right!" he said. "You boys wear bibs and play this end. You others play without bibs at the far end of the pitch. The side ready first will kick off."

Jimmy had, to his delight, been selected as a striker. Luke and Brendan were both playing on the other side in midfield for the 'bibs'. Jimmy's team were ready first, so would kick off. Jimmy's co-striker suggested that Jimmy took the kick-off and passed to him, which Jimmy was all too happy to do.

He gave a short pass. *The boots felt good.* The other boy ran a few paces before sending the ball down for the right-winger to run on to. The winger, a boy with considerable speed, received the ball and sprinted down past the opposing full-back before sending over a low cross. Jimmy's co-striker was a fraction late in getting to the ball, and it fell conveniently to Jimmy.

It was a perfect first touch. The goal beckoned, with just the keeper to beat. Eyes on the ball, and the cleanest strike drove the ball low to the keeper's right and into the net. A sweet moment.

As Jimmy ran back to the centre circle, loudly applauded by his team, he knew that was the sweetest strike he had ever produced – *the boots were perfect.*

But the 'bibs' fought back, and within five minutes they had taken the lead, one of their goals being scored from distance by a tall, athletic boy called Kevin. Jimmy's team had a game on their hands!

The rest of the half was evenly balanced, and Mr. Smith made a quick turnaround with just a short break for drinks.

Jimmy's strike partner was called Carl, and although immy reckoned Carl was a far better player than he was, it still felt as if they were working well together and that they may well score further goals. The boots were feeling great, and Jimmy just wanted to play and play.

Sure enough, within ten minutes both Carl and Jimmy had scored. Jimmy's was a simple tap-in, but Carl's was a scorcher. So, Jimmy's team was now leading 3-2.

It was 'nip-and-tuck' after that, with both teams striking the woodwork and their keepers making good saves. But with five minutes to go, the 'bibs' produced a superb attack which resulted in Kevin netting his second goal. 3-3.

*Within moments Jimmy and Kai had locked
horns in an ugly brawl.*

Both teams now were fighting for the winning goal. Each had worthy attempts, with Jimmy having a shot cleared off the line. So close to a hat-trick!

Then, with just two minutes left, the 'bibs' launched a strong attack down the right flank. Jimmy, not wanting his team to concede a late decider, was quickly back helping out in defence. The ball was swung in from the right and was met beautifully on the volley by a tall, lanky boy, Kai Stevens, an attacking midfielder for the 'bibs'. The ball was speeding towards the goal, away from the keeper. But it struck Jimmy on the shoulder and deflected off for a corner – much to the annoyance of Kai.

"Aw, that was a handball, ref!" came out of his lips. But it was a stifled protest – he did not really want Mr. Smith to hear him. Whether the coach heard or not, he simply signalled for a corner to be taken.

The 'bibs' winger went across to take the corner. Jimmy found himself marking Kai, the boy whose shot he had blocked. The corner was taken, and as the ball came over, Kai muttered, *"That was handball,"* and elbowed Jimmy in the ribs. Jimmy, without thinking, hit back at Kai, who immediately gave a loud yell. Within moments the two had locked horns in an ugly brawl.

Smithy blew the whistle and walked over to the fighting boys. "Both of you, stop at once!" No raised voice – just very, very firm.

The others looked on with concern.

Finally the two boys stopped fighting.

"Come here, the two of you," he ordered, standing a few feet away.

The boys walked over to the coach. Jimmy, head down, was inwardly fuming for having let himself down. No way would he stand a chance of making the team now. Put simply, *he had blown it.*

Kai was glaring accusingly at Jimmy. He was still seething.

"Go and wait on opposite touchlines, the two of you," ordered the coach. "Your game is over."

The two boys made it over to their respective touchlines, and the coach resumed the game.

Shortly afterwards, Mr. Smith blew for full-time, with the scores still level at 3-3.

The coach ordered the teams to change their boots and gather behind the far goal mouth. He then called Kai and Jimmy to himself.

"You both actually played well," he stated. "Unfortunately you have blotted your copybooks, as we say. Have you anything to say for yourselves?"

"I'm sorry, sir. I shouldn't have retaliated," replied Jimmy. He nervously waited for the coach's next words.

"And what have *you* to say for yourself?" asked the coach, addressing Kai.

Kai did not reply.

"Well, boys," he continued, "the first thing I require of any players in my team is acceptable conduct. You would be playing in a team, and so you would need to be able to get on with one another."

Jimmy was really kicking himself for losing his rag. But then he thought, *Actually, Kai was totally out of order.*

"Well," resumed the coach, "we all have to get home someday. So this is what I have decided: Kai – I actually heard your accusation directed at Jimmy. I also clearly saw you were the aggressor. Jimmy did not handle the ball, and even if he had done, you had no right to hit him. As things stand, Kai Stevens, you are highly unlikely to be considered for the team to play St. Mary's on Wednesday. Jimmy," he continued, "you should not have fought back – you know that. It is for the person in charge to sort out any problems.

But you have apologised, which is good. I shall review your position regarding the team over the next few days. But what you must realise is this: your actions, as well as Kai's, have been witnessed today by all these boys, many of whom will hope to be selected for the school football team. I shall therefore be expecting something extra from you over the next week, to make up for letting yourself down today. I shall be checking with your teachers to see how you have responded before selecting the team to play St. Mary's. Now, both of you quickly change your boots and join the other boys."

As he made his way home after football practice, Jimmy knew he had let himself down. He had lost his rag – far worse, it now seemed, than losing any match. But he was determined to make up for it.

Then, as he thought back to the coach's words, something struck him which was encouraging to him: "I shall be expecting something extra from you…" That was more positive than what some of his teachers used to say to him: "You'd better keep out of trouble," or, "Watch your behaviour." Those words simply scared him. They meant he dared not put a foot wrong; everywhere he went was like treading on egg shells. But Smithy's words gave Jimmy a rather different feeling. After all, he was a new boy and desperately keen to give it a go at Graysfield. He didn't want to be going to school every morning like a frightened rabbit. He wanted to get the best out of his time there. And Smithy's words seemed to give him the opportunity to do just that.

Something extra, he thought. *Well, why not?*

He wasn't quite sure if he could keep it up for a whole day, let alone a week. But he would give it a go.

7

SOMETHING EXTRA

Jimmy decided he would have to tell his mum what had happened at the football practice. He found it hard, almost impossible, to keep anything from her, and she was likely to find out anyway. Besides, in a way it might help. So when Mum asked how school had gone that day, he came right out with it.

"Yes, you must have been really mad when he hit you. I'm sure I would have been," said Mum.

That meant a lot to Jimmy. His mum had, in her younger days, been quite a player in the county hockey team. To hear her sympathising like this was a real help.

"Yes, I've had times like that myself," she admitted, "and when I was younger I sometimes *did* respond. But it never helped. The trouble is, when a red mist comes over you, I know it's often hard to do anything else."

Talking it over with Mum was certainly helping. It had clearly been the right move to tell her. She was able to see Jimmy's situation through her own past experiences.

"I had to learn the hard way," said Mum. "Like you, I was no pushover. If someone had a go at me, I tended instinctively to hit back – sometimes literally. But I soon realised that never achieved anything. Other teams will soon knew if you get easily riled, and they can sometimes play on it – you know, get awarded easy free kicks, penalties or, worse, a sending off. It is difficult, but if you can hold yourself together, you'll become a better player also."

This was helpful. Jimmy already knew that Mum had been a fine and respected hockey player in her younger days. Both Dad and Uncle Reg had said so, and on a rare occasion when Mum had asked Jimmy to fetch something from her room, he had noticed a photograph of her in her hockey-playing days. But he hadn't heard about her 'red mist' days. She had clearly turned things around. Well, if Mum could make things happen, then why couldn't he?

Maybe there was still hope for him after all.

Jimmy thanked his mum for her help. He was really hoping he wouldn't have too many 'Kai' situations to deal with again, but it had been good to talk things through, and Jimmy did believe that his mum's words would be of value to him someday. Her part-time cleaning job often made it difficult for her to attend school functions. But she was always around to give him support – especially when he needed it most.

The immediate challenge was to make it into the team against St. Mary's. As he understood it, Mr. Smith was saying he might be good enough to play in the team, but his retaliation against Kai had threatened his place. In some way he had to make up for that before Mr. Smith posted the team next week.

Well, as Mum had always advised, he would do his best.

Jimmy challenged himself to give it a real go every lesson, however boring or challenging the lesson may appear to be. It would probably be difficult, but it could make the difference between playing and not playing in the team.

Besides – you never knew, it might even make the lessons a shade less unbearable.

First up on Friday morning was maths. The lesson was actually not too bad, because this was still the first fortnight of term and so Miss Bennett gave them a mini-test on work they would have covered in primary school.

Jimmy reasoned that he must know how to tackle at least some of the questions. So he did give it a go. And he actually managed to score half marks, with fifteen out of thirty. *It could have been worse,* he thought.

Then it was double English with Mr. Sweeney. Jimmy was in luck. The teacher produced a comprehension passage from *War Horse.* How good was that, since Jimmy had seen the film just a month ago with his friend Gary Thomas from his old school! This helped him understand the passage much better, so he was able to answer most of the questions. Hopefully he would achieve a good mark when the books were handed back next week.

Geography after break was map work – and Jimmy regarded himself as pretty hopeless at that. But he did give it a go. And it paid off. Mr. Coombes could see he was trying hard, and gave him a merit award for effort.

After all that, lunch was a sweet reward: chicken drumsticks, chips and peas, followed by syrup sponge and custard, went down very well, thank you!

And one thing which hadn't changed from primary school was lunchtime 'footy' with Luke and Brendan. In fact, if anything it was better. There was more space, and the pitches were bigger. It had also been an opportunity to make new friends. Charlie was a tall lad who Jimmy reckoned would walk it into the football team. He always played after lunch, and seemed quite a decent guy. Then there was Ravi. He was always smiling, and quite a joker. Not bad at 'footy' either.

Afternoon classes on Friday included double Art. This was the only subject Jimmy had not yet had at Graysfield, and he was just hoping he might find something in it to get him interested.

The teacher was Mr. Harris. And as soon as the children entered the Art room everyone noticed a difference. Mr. Harris was not at his desk. He was seated in the centre of the room at an easel, and seemingly immersed in some absorbing artwork of his own. He silently indicated to everyone to gather round either side of him to have a look.

8

GETTING THE PICTURE

At first it was unclear what Mr. Harris was painting. His brushes – for he worked rapidly with first one brush then another – appeared to be criss-crossing an indeterminate space on the paper with greys, yellows and browns. As the class watched, in a very short period of time the painting became a typical Cornish harbour at twilight, with fishing boats in place and locals depicted enjoying their evening cod and chips, with the sun slowly setting behind the distant hills.

Jimmy was hooked. Before his very eyes, Mr. Harris had demonstrated to the class what could be produced with paint and brush – and barely a word spoken!

"Now that's genius," mused Jimmy. "Pure genius."

Then Mr. Harris rose from his stool. "Welcome!" he greeted everyone. "Please be seated."

Within a further five minutes he had convinced everyone bar none that they too could produce something of which they could be proud.

The class had been discussing Mr. Harris's painting. "It seemed to come out of nothing, sir," said Joseph, a small bespectacled lad with fair hair.

"What I'd like you to do," said Mr. Harris warmly, "is try to draw something which expresses your feelings, something inside you. You may wish to reflect your mood, or how things are with you at the present time. Use your pencil lightly first, to get the basic idea. Firm it up as your idea becomes clearer. Then the colours – pale, pastel shades first; any bold colours later. Don't be afraid to sit and have a think before you start. Enjoy!"

For a moment Jimmy's head was swimming. But he was going to have a real try, that was for certain.

You may wish to reflect your mood or how things are with you? Well, to be honest, thought Jimmy, *I am feeling pretty uneasy, really... I want to do well so that I can get into the team. I really do.*

He sat for a while, considering.

Then he picked up his pencil and began to draw – tentatively at first, with short, faint pencil strokes around the sides and base of the paper. As he continued, he felt he was growing in confidence, and his pencil strokes became firmer and more defined. Shortly after, he felt he was ready to start painting.

He remembered Mr. Harris's words, "Begin with pale, pastel colours." For a moment he was a little confused. As he had been drawing, it had become clear to Jimmy that his artwork was indeed reflecting his mood; his pencil marks and now his brushstrokes were representing a dark place, a sort of forest. So pale colours seemed not to help. But he kept going. Then another theme entered his head. The paper was filling up – yes, with pencil marks and pale paint strokes criss-crossing much of the sheet. But Jimmy now was focussing on another aspect – something which was to make the whole picture make sense.

The boy continued painting. Criss-cross brush strokes of a whitish-grey, then pale yellow-green, then a hint of pale beige or brown. The tones were gradually becoming less pale, deepening into the hues of a forest. But still a space near the top right-hand corner remained clear.

Jimmy put down his brush and surveyed his picture. Then he closed his eyes for a moment.

I shall get through it, he thought. *I really will.*

He picked up a clean brush and dipped the tip into the white paint and put some on his palate. He then dipped the brush in the yellow and mixed it with the white. Satisfied, he carefully but confidently painted a faint point of light near the top right corner of his painting. He then filled most of the rest of the paper with 'forest'.

One thing remained to be done.

Near the bottom left corner he made a bold attempt at the small, shadowy figure of a boy, almost but not totally immersed in the darkness of the forest trees.

That's me, he thought.

He cleaned his brushes, sat back in his seat and closed his eyes.

Yes, he thought, *that's me. And I shall come through this. That's for sure.*

———————

"It's time to pack up now, Jimmy."

Mr. Harris had actually noticed Jimmy before his classmates had. Quite astonishing really, since there wasn't much that escaped them. But Mr. Harris was an observant man, and a particularly compassionate teacher. He noticed everything that went on – particularly the pupils who were putting in a good deal of effort.

He had watched Jimmy working on his picture. He had noticed the thought, the effort – and the pauses. He had seen the picture take shape and, most of all, he had seen it take on meaning. He reckoned Jimmy should feel pleased with his efforts. He wasn't that surprised when he noticed him actually nod off.

He had got up to tell Jimmy that is was time to get ready to go. "And I do like your painting," he added encouragingly.

How good is that! A teacher saying he likes my painting, thought Jimmy. He thanked Mr. Harris and gave a quiet "Yes-s-s!" before clearing his place ready to leave the room.

"A good day," Jimmy muttered to himself as he left school shortly after. "Yes, a really good day."

9

THE MUSIC SHOP

Matthew Jones was a mild-mannered boy in Jimmy's class with an interest in music. All kinds, really. When he was eight he had heard a young trumpeter on a TV talent show, and he decided there and then he must have a trumpet. On his ninth birthday he got his wish when his parents gave him a trumpet as a joint present, and he had been smitten ever since.

Most Saturdays, Matthew loved nothing better than going down town with his family and spending time in one of the town's many music shops before meeting up with them at a snack bar or restaurant. One of Matthew's favourite venues was 'Mick's Music', a true 'Aladdin's cave' of all things musical. Matthew's parents had bought his trumpet there, since they sold all kinds of brass and woodwind instruments, as well as drums, guitars and plenty of stringed and percussion instruments.

But that was not all. Downstairs there was a vast store of CDs and DVDs covering every type of music. And to cap it all, there was even a very popular Vinyl section, where music buffs could spend ages rummaging for old treasures!

Jimmy had noticed when Matthew had signed up for the music club on Wednesdays, and it was then that Matthew had told him about his trumpet. Jimmy did have a slight interest in music – his dad had briefly been a member of a little-known group in his younger days – and so when

Matthew had asked him if he would like to go down with him on Saturday to 'Mick's Music', Jimmy had promptly agreed.

Matthew's dad had a morning conference in town, and so had arranged to pick up Jimmy at nine o'clock sharp. Jimmy was well ready, and enjoyed the ride down to a part of the town he rarely visited.

Mr. Jones parked up and set off for his conference. Matthew's mum suggested to the boys that they could have a good time in 'Mick's Music' while she and older sister Catherine visited the clothes shops. They would come back for the boys in an hour before all meeting up with Dad later.

Jimmy followed Matthew through the crowded streets, past inviting shop fronts and busy traffic. It was all fascinating to Jimmy, who had been brought up in a much quieter part of town.

They came to an area of specialist shops. Bakers, butchers and newsagents had given way to shops selling books, old paintings, all kinds of collectors' items – and music shops. And there was 'Mick's Music', with an amazing display of musical instruments for all to enjoy.

Matthew led the way into the shop and made a beeline for the 'Music for Brass' section. Jimmy watched as he flicked through several books before selecting one.

Jimmy was already in love with this shop. He was particularly fascinated by a row of brightly coloured guitars displayed attractively before him. But music would have to wait. At present football was his priority, and he simply couldn't wait to make his mark in that.

Matthew paid for his book and suggested they went downstairs to the CD and Vinyl sections. Jimmy didn't really know what vinyl was, but he followed Matthew to see what further delights this amazing shop had to offer.

10

MARTIN

Martin had had a chequered past. A bright lad, at eighteen he had won a university scholarship in music, where he had also been a keen sportsman. He had enjoyed playing rugby and cricket, but his special love was football, through which he had won several prized trophies.

While still in his first year, his aunt, whose large house he had once visited, had died, leaving him a large sum of money in her will. Aunt Ruby had married into money but had never had children. Two years later her husband Ronnie had died, and Ruby had decided to downsize. But her health had taken a turn for the worse before she could get the wheels in motion, and so she had remained in her large house until her passing.

The distance from her sister's home had not helped, though she had always taken a keen interest in Martin's progress, firmly believing he would do well in life. Her latest will stipulated that her house and land would be sold, with the proceeds going to her sister – except that a lump sum of £100,000 from the estate was to be passed to Martin, to set him up for his future.

Martin, already high on university life, now saw the bequest as the answer to all his dreams. Always a bit of an extrovert, he began to visit all the fashion stores in town, determined to look good wherever he might go. He also began to frequent expensive restaurants and pricey country pubs – at total odds with his previous penny-pinching student life.

One day he was passing a car showroom when he noticed a superb second-hand sports car. He had already delved deep into his aunt's inheritance, but the sparkling beauty he saw before him was a very alluring attraction. No, he no longer had enough left to afford to buy the car, but what if he were to gamble a thousand pounds in order to win, say, *ten thousand* pounds or more towards the car? There would be plenty of betting companies on the high street or online who would be only too glad to accept his money. So he gave it a go.

Sadly, and not really surprisingly, his first gamble was unsuccessful – as was his second, and his third. Within two weeks he had shelled out nearly ten thousand pounds on ill-advised punts – and he was now just starting to get a little worried. But still, the nagging thought remained: *One good, successful bet could win enough to buy the car; it could even get me back towards the security of several months ago.*

He was passing the betting shop close by his 'digs' in town. They were offering odds of 10-1 against Rising Star at Aintree. By this time he had been studying horses, and was convinced that Rising Star had a better than evens chance of winning this race. It was worth a punt.

He was down to his last two thousand pounds of spare cash. Plenty for a student – in fact, ridiculous money for most. But he reckoned, if it was going to be a winner – as he was convinced it would be – he might as well bet enough to make a big difference. He would bet one thousand five hundred pounds. That would still leave five hundred pounds – he could easily live on that together with his student loan. But he wasn't going to lose anyway, he told himself. It was certainly worth the gamble. He went in and paid his stake. Then he waited eagerly for the race on the screens.

The sparkling car Martin saw before him was a very alluring attraction.

Rising Star was doing well. With three furlongs to go, the horse was clear by two lengths, and looking a good bet to win the race. Martin could hardly contain himself. But with little more than two furlongs remaining, an unfancied horse, Cornish Prince, came up fast on the outside and was seriously threatening the leader. Rising Star skilfully managed to fend off the challenge and for a while seemed to have done enough for victory. But the extra effort took its toll, and the final six hundred yards proved too much. Cornish Prince came neck-and-neck with just two hundred yards to go – and then relentlessly ground on towards the finishing line.

Rising Star made a great effort. But it wasn't enough. The final sprint of Cornish Prince had proved decisive, and Martin's horse finished fifth behind a cluster of other challengers.

Martin was crushed. His sports car dream was over. He returned, totally deflated, to his 'digs'.

As Martin entered his house, there were three envelopes on the doormat, one of which bore an ominous red border. His heart sank even lower than before.

He opened the envelope and was reminded, to his horror, that he had begun buying items online and on credit when funds had begun to dip. It was a bill from one of his favourite menswear stores, Man-about-Town. Martin stared in stunned silence at the red rim around the bill and the amount to pay: £969.50.

He slumped into a chair, lay back and closed his eyes for a moment. His mind was a blur. How had it come to this?

Then, as he opened his eyes again, his gaze was drawn to a photograph on his bookshelf, one that he had put there at the start of his university course. It was a photo of his mother. How thrilled she had been when he had won a scholarship. "You're the first in the family to do anything like that," she had said. "We're all wishing you well."

For a second time, he closed his eyes. Yes, the family had wished him well: his dad, who had recently set up his own painting and decorating business; his mum, a hard-working part-time cleaner; his younger brother Jason; and, of course, his gran.

He reached into his pocket and took out his wallet, removing a small photograph. *Gran.* Martin looked steadily at her face. She had always been very close to Martin. She always told him he was her first boy, since Mum had been her only child. Martin had had a very special relationship with her.

He looked again at the photo. Gran's face showed character, with a hint of sadness. Her husband, a Baptist church minister, had died before Martin had been born, and she had managed on her own ever since. Life had not been easy, but she had always tried to remain cheerful. But it was also a kind and generous face. To Martin it showed affection and love. She had always been proud of him and keen to hear how he was doing.

A tear came to his eye. He had not contacted Gran since Christmas – other things had taken over. So it was now several months since he had even spoken to her.

But how could he contact her now? No way could he tell her about his situation, his problems or all that had led up to his present woeful state.

He sat in stunned silence. This was bad. Really bad. What could he do? He really, honestly did not know.

He glanced again at his gran's photo. An honest face. Fun, too. But also serious. He had valued her friendship, her affection. As he had grown up, it had meant a lot to him.

Then he remembered something about her which strangely seemed to resonate with his present situation. Whenever the family had experienced tough times or things had not been going so well, Gran had remained strong. Where others might falter, she had been a rock, one on which everyone could rely. Many times when Martin had been sick as a child or when things had been tough at school, Gran would say, "I'm praying for you." And as far as Martin could remember, it had worked every time.

He sat a while longer pondering. It had worked. *But then,* thought Martin, *I was a child. Was it not easier to believe then? I'm older now. Nearly said "wiser". Mmm... perhaps not as wise as all that.*

He looked again at Gran's photo. Honesty, fun... and wisdom. Yes, wisdom. *She* was certainly wise. Her advice, not just to Martin, but to other family members, had proved good time and time again.

He thought again of her words, "I'm praying for you." She believed in prayer. It worked for her. It was a meaningful part of her life. Maybe...? *Nah, don't be daft, Martin. You don't need... After all, you control your own destiny.*

He found himself repeating the words, "You control your—" This time he almost choked on his own words. He slammed the arms of his chair.

"YOU'VE MESSED UP, YOU FOOL!" he yelled. "BIG TIME MESSED IT UP!"

He felt like throwing something at the window. Or at the TV screen. But by this time, he had retrieved just enough of his judgement to realise it would only make matters worse.

"No! You've got to work this one out," he said to himself. "You've got to do something positive to try and get your life back on the right track."

He then remembered words he had long forgotten – words his gran had spoken to him after he had got into trouble once at school. He had nicked a boy's Switch – and thought he had got away with it. But his mum spotted the games console in his room and made him give it back. Mum and Dad were furious, but Gran prayed. "That's all very well," Dad said to her, "but he's got to learn right from wrong," and he blocked Martin's pocket money for a month *as well as* making him write a letter of apology to the owner of the Switch. Gran simply said to Martin, as usual, "I shall be praying for you."

All Martin knew about the incident after that was that the boy whose console he had stolen thanked him for his letter, and three weeks later told Martin that his parents had decided not to press charges.

It had never even occurred to Martin that the police might be involved.

As he now recalled his gran's influence for good on his early life, Martin knew one thing for sure: he couldn't carry on as he was going.

Yes, he would need time. Time to take it all in – this horrid mess he had got himself into. And time to work out what to do to put things right.

Martin suddenly felt ashamed. His gran – as well as his mum and dad – had had such high hopes for him. And what had he done? He had blown it. Wasted his aunt's inheritance and, because of his reckless lifestyle, had all but ruined his university career. He was in no mood to continue the course, and even if he did, he had no confidence that he would now succeed. He decided there and then that he would have to pull out. Yes, regrets – *big* regrets. Mainly, letting down his family. But as he saw it now, it was the only way. Yes, he would phone the office in the morning to apologise profusely and tell them his decision.

Martin sat gazing at his gran's photo, recalling the love and kindness, humour and advice she had showered on him. He suddenly felt deeply ashamed. He had let her down. All her hopes for him, her pride in him, he had shredded it, ignored it. His parents too. Maybe they were less demonstrative, but Martin knew they too cared deeply for him. How saddened all three would be if they were to know about his present situation. Yes, he had messed up big time.

He could see now this was the rapid road to ruin. Sure, deep down he knew that all three – Mum, Dad and Gran – were forgiving people who would try to help him out of this hole. But that, Martin reckoned, must be a last option. He must do all he could to reform his life and reconstruct it on his own.

Then he had an idea. He had been close friends at school with Ralph. Ralph had wanted to set up a rock group but had never quite made it. Ralph's father, totally crazy about many kinds of music, had done really well in setting up a music shop in town – 'Mick's Music', it was called. He sold everything from cellos and piccolos to guitars and drums. It really was the place to go if you were into music. And it was going well.

Martin still loved his music – classic, jazz, pop, you name it. More importantly at present, he needed to earn some money. He had messed up his university career. Yes, he regretted that bitterly. But he must show a bit of spine, and dig himself out of this. He had always got on well with Ralph. They had kept in touch since leaving school. He knew he would be able to work alongside him in his father's store. But did his dad need him – or want him? Only one way to find out…

Martin still had Ralph's number. He picked up his phone and took the plunge.

And yes, he did breathe just a little prayer.

11

A Fresh Start

The way Ralph greeted Martin that afternoon, you'd think they were long-lost brothers.

"Hi, Martin ! What a surprise! How's it going?"

It was actually almost three years since they had parted company, following GCSEs at school. Martin had then gone into the sixth form, while Ralph had taken a course at the local college. Ralph was now helping his dad in his music business, while still looking out for anything else that might come his way. And then came the question Martin had dreaded:

"How's life at Oxford?"

Martin, although ringing on a sort of impulse, had at least had the presence of mind to prepare one or two answers to awkward questions. He was not going to lie, but he felt no need to tell the whole sorry saga, certainly not at this stage, to someone whom he wanted to help him out.

"It's not worked out," admitted Martin. "I messed up, really. Not knuckled down. Blown it." Then, after a short pause, "But I've realised how stupid I've been. And I'm determined to make a fresh start."

All this was a shock to Ralph, so he didn't twig where Martin was leading. "So what you gonna do now? Or are you just looking?"

Martin decided he may as well come straight to the point. "I need to earn some dosh," he confessed. "Don't s'pose you know anyone or anywhere I might try?"

Ralph paused a moment, then said, "As it happens, Hilda's leaving us in the summer. She's been with us for years. Taken charge of our Retro and Vinyl section. Don't think Dad's found anyone to replace her yet. You'd need training. But I could help with that. D'you want me to have a word with the old man?"

Martin was almost too excited for words. But he did manage to blurt out, "Wow, yes! That would be great, if you could. I reckon I'd love that. Sounds perfect."

"Leave it with me," confirmed Ralph. "You know Dad. He's pretty decent. And he likes you. Could be a winner!"

Martin had a fleeting involuntary thought: *I've had enough of 'winners'!* But he managed to stifle it before it passed his lips.

"I'll speak to Dad after work," promised Ralph. "I'll phone you tonight, just to let you know his response. Don't expect an instant yes, but hopefully it won't be a no. Anyway, I'll give you a call."

To say Martin was relieved was a massive understatement. He thanked his friend repeatedly before hanging up and going off to prepare himself some kind of a meal.

Just before half-past-seven, Martin had a call from Ralph.

"I've spoken to Dad," he began cheerily, "and he's up for it. Obviously, he's got to see how you do first, so he says you can come along and shadow Hilda before she leaves us. So you can be helping out and getting some kind of pay. Then when she leaves, if all is going well, Dad reckons he can work something out more permanently."

Martin was on Cloud Nine. "When can I start?" he asked eagerly.

"Dad says pop in tomorrow for a chat. And come prepared to stay the day if you both hit it off!"

Martin was definitely up for this challenge. This time he would not mess up. He would grasp the opportunity with both hands. "See you tomorrow then," he promised, as he finished the call. He felt like a schoolboy. He simply couldn't wait for tomorrow. And this time, he was determined to give it his all.

12

THE GRAYSFIELD LINK

At first Jimmy was less impressed with the downstairs section than with what he had seen above. Boxes of old records were not really his thing, although Matthew did seem perfectly at home here. Jimmy watched fascinated, as his friend checked out dozens of old numbers, clearly looking for a particular item. Finally he turned to the young assistant nearby.

"I'm looking for pieces I can play on my trumpet," he said. "Anything. Classical, jazz, I don't care. What have you got?"

"So glad you asked," replied the young man. "I love brass." He moved swiftly along to a section Matthew had yet to examine. Almost immediately he plucked out a small vinyl record. "Here, try this," he said. "One of the all-time greats. And one of my favourites."

Matthew took hold of the record and read the label. "*Midnight in Moscow* – Kenny Ball… Yes, my dad likes him. I don't know the piece, but I might try it."

"I'll play it for you," offered the assistant, swiftly turning to a music centre behind the shop counter.

A few seconds later the record had started. For an old record it was clear enough. Within seconds Matthew was hooked. He stood entranced, then started fingering imaginary notes in front of his face as if he were the soloist.

Jimmy, too, soon caught the bug. "You must buy it," he said. "I'd love to hear you having a go at that."

Matthew needed no persuasion. "Of course, I'd need the sheet music; do you have it in stock?" he asked.

"Sure have," replied the assistant as he moved along and picked a book from a nearby shelf. "*Tunes for Young Trumpeters*," he said. "Just the job!"

Matthew was ecstatic. The assistant bagged book and record, and Matthew paid.

"See you like 'footy'…" remarked the assistant, eyeing Jimmy's junior school football shirt as he waited with his friend at the counter.

"Yes, I'm hoping to get into my new school team."

"And which school is that?" enquired the young man, interested.

"Graysfield," replied Jimmy. "That's why I went there really. 'Cos of the football."

The shop assistant laughed. "Know what?" he chuckled. "I went to Graysfield too for the same reason. Loved it." Then, thoughtfully, he added, "Is Smithy still there? The games teacher. Mr. Smith? I got on well with him."

"Oh yes, he is!" replied Jimmy immediately.

"Could you tell him, if he ever wants help with the football, I'd love to assist. I've got my football coaching certificate and would be really happy to help out!"

Jimmy promised he would tell 'Smithy', and the assistant handed him a small card.

"My details are on there, including my mobile phone number."

Jimmy thanked him for the card, and the two boys went back upstairs and out of the shop before returning home with Matthew's family.

The following Monday morning, at the beginning of P.E., Jimmy handed Smithy the card from the shop assistant.

The head of games looked at the card, thanked Jimmy and seemed particularly interested. "Hmm… Martin Davis?" he muttered. "With his skills he should make a good football coach. And it could be an opportunity to arrange more fixtures."

Later that day he had a word with the headmaster, and within a month the headmaster had interviewed the music shop assistant, carrying out all necessary checks, and agreed that he should help with the football out of official school hours.

Martin was delighted by this. Thanks to Mick's Music, Martin had restarted his life, and now he had just longed for something fun to do in his free time. So returning to Graysfield was a dream come true. He quickly settled into Smithy's routine, and soon built up a good rapport with the young footballers, particularly those unlikely to make the 'A' team.

13

THE NOTICEBOARD

It was the day before the Big Match. Importantly, it was the day when Smithy would announce the team for the match. How Jimmy wanted to be in that team! He hurried over to the noticeboard, where a crowd of boys had already gathered.

The list had been placed high up so that everyone could easily read it, but from where Jimmy stood behind two tall boys, he was unable to see the names. He waited patiently until the queue died down a little, then moved forward to read the list. *And he re-read it.* Three times Jimmy read the list before he could admit to himself that his name was not there.

Jimmy was more than a little disappointed. But he wasn't going to hang around there risking others seeing how he felt. He turned and moved towards his form room.

Would you believe it, the first person he saw on his way down the corridor was Brendan.

"Well done, Bren!" Jimmy made himself say the words, though he really wanted to add, "Only wish I was playing alongside you."

Brendan thanked Jimmy and added, "You've still got a chance, Jimmy."

"What d'you mean?" replied Jimmy, puzzled.

"Didn't you read the full notice? There were only ten names on the sheet. That means one more player and a sub are yet

Brendan added, "You've still got a chance, Jimmy."

to be named. And that's what Smithy said at the bottom of the team sheet."

Jimmy admitted he hadn't read beyond the list of names. He was perplexed though. Why should Mr. Smith do that? Unless...

He looked at Brendan. They exchanged knowing glances. Yes, that was it. The two names that might have hoped to be listed were Jimmy and Kai Stevens, the guy he had fallen out with at last week's training session. Maybe they were still being made to sweat it out and prove themselves on account of what had happened then. Still some hope then?

Jimmy did not have to wait long for an answer to his question. As he rounded the corner of the corridor, he saw Mr. Smith outside his form room talking to his tutor, Mr. Knight. As Jimmy drew near, Mr. Smith glanced momentarily at him before closing his conversation with, "Speak to you later, then," after which he abruptly strode off down the corridor.

Jimmy was so keen to know why the head of games had been talking to his form tutor. Was it anything to do with him and his issue with Kai last week?

"Morning, Jimmy. I'd like a word with you, please," said Mr. Knight, as Jimmy approached.

His tutor explained that Mr. Smith was keeping Jimmy's place in the team open until the afternoon, when he would have another word with the tutor. The final decision would depend on Jimmy's continued efforts and attitude in the classroom and around the school during that time. So he would still be watched closely.

Jimmy was determined not to miss out at this final stage. This was his big chance. He *must* get it right.

The early part of the day passed smoothly enough. First up was double English with Mr. Sweeney, and Jimmy managed to achieve a 'well done' for a character portrait of his mate Luke, as well as a merit for his *War Horse* comprehension. Final lesson before break was Music, and Jimmy, still excited by his visit to Mick's Music at the weekend, was delighted when he twice came in right on time with his cymbals for the final *clash* of the class's latest home-made composition.

So far so good...

Jimmy hurried off at breaktime to the tuck shop before making his way outside, hoping to meet up with Brendan and Luke.

14

TROUBLE BREWING

Jimmy's mates were not around yet. He looked around. The only person close by was little Tommy Newton, who was propped against a wall, peeling an orange.

Jimmy looked further out and saw quite a few boys over by the basketball pitch. And right at the front was Kai Stevens – together with his special mate, Bobby Ford, a boy Jimmy believed to have a sharp temper.

Jimmy's relationship with Kai since the showdown at the football practice had not been easy, to say the least. Kai, although still hoping for a place in the team, knew deep down that he had a far slimmer chance of making it than Jimmy. The coach had made that clear. But as far as he was concerned, the worst possible outcome would be for Jimmy to be selected and for him to be left out. No, that would be too much. Jimmy, being perceptive, sensed that Kai might be thinking along these lines, and was therefore trying hard to avoid any tricky situation.

I must keep away from them, thought Jimmy. *The last thing I want is trouble.* But his heart sank when he saw that Bobby had noticed him. Bobby nudged Kai, and the two of them started walking towards him.

Having just come out of the building, the only direction Jimmy could take to move away from the two boys was back inside – and being a fine day, that was not allowed; he would get into trouble if he went back in, and that was certainly not what he wanted. So he paused, hoping Kai and Bobby would just stay away.

The boys, however, were moving slowly but directly towards him.

Jimmy wanted no trouble, but he was not a runner. No way was he going to run away from anyone, especially Bobby Ford. The two boys were only steps away now. Then, as they approached, Bobby changed direction slightly and nudged into Jimmy, knocking him slightly aside.

Jimmy was not one to be pushed around, so with little thought he regained his balance and gave a similar barge to Bobby. Almost immediately, though, he wished he hadn't. Bobby lurched suddenly and theatrically to the side, and then dropped dramatically to the ground, wailing as if in shock and great pain. He fell conveniently close to a flower bed, and Jimmy, ever observant, noticed Bobby slyly pressing his right hand into the soggy soil. The boy then rolled over as if in agony, allowing his face to fall on to his muddy hand. By the time he rolled back, his face was plastered in mud.

Give him an Oscar! thought Jimmy, at the same time now expecting trouble ahead.

Miss Britton, the duty teacher, hearing the rumpus, had hurried over. "Oh my goodness, what have we here?" she began. "Now, you boys must look where you're going, you know."

"He shoved me, miss," blubbered Bobby. "Shoved me into the rose bushes."

"It's a wonder you're not scratched to pieces then, I must say," remarked Miss Britton.

Bobby was now wondering whether he might just have done better by deliberately giving himself a slight scratch with a rose thorn. But he decided he would have to make the most of things as they were.

"It were 'im, miss. Jimmy Evans. Always messing about, 'e is, miss."

Miss Britton did not directly teach any of the three boys, but she certainly had heard the name 'Jimmy Evans'. In fact, this morning Mr. Smith, noticing she was on break duty, had mentioned the names of the two boys, Jimmy and Kai, who were 'on probation' before tomorrow's big match.

"Jimmy Evans, eh?" Miss Britton seized on the name like a detective chalking up their first catch.

Jimmy did not want to answer, but what good would that do?

"Yes, miss..." he mumbled.

"Right," declared Miss Britton, suddenly deciding on an action plan. "You" – pointing to Kai – "take your friend in to First Aid for a mop-up. And I," she said threateningly, turning to Jimmy, "shall report you to Mr. Smith. I know this isn't the first time you've been in trouble lately."

The teacher looked on as Kai made a right meal of arm-lifting Bobby towards the First Aid room, before moving back to deal with another group of children involved in a petty squabble.

Kai cast a sickening grin over his shoulder towards Jimmy as he departed, leaving Jimmy ruing his luck and dreading the next meeting with his coach.

15

SHOWDOWN WITH SMITHY

As Jimmy arrived at the dining hall for lunch, there was Mr. Smith to meet him.

"Jimmy, I would be grateful if you would come to see me in my room off the sports hall after you've had your lunch, please."

That was it. No extras. No need for threats or raising of voice or intimidating comments. The head of games was strict, but he was fair also. Jimmy was therefore really hoping that Mr. Smith would listen to him, and that he would be given the opportunity to give his side of the incident in the playground that morning.

He polished off his beef lasagne with chips with greater energy, now that he had seen his coach – if only as a preliminary to their main meeting. He then enjoyed a strawberry trifle and a swig of water before making his way to the sports hall. Nervous yet hopeful.

Colin Smith was an experienced secondary school teacher who had, in his earlier years, played football at a high level for a northern non-league club. He had grown up in East Lancashire, and his upbringing had been tough. Many a day, his parents had gone without food in order to ensure that the children had enough to eat. So life had been hard. But Colin had learnt a lot, benefiting from the selflessness and dedication of his parents, who had never failed to put their children before themselves.

His parents had long since passed away, both deaths arguably due (at least in part) to the difficult life choices they had had to make. They had bequeathed their tough, unselfish spirit to their children, especially Colin, the eldest, who from an early age had seen them as his guiding light. By the time his football career had come to an early end, his mother had already died, but his father keenly supported his efforts to take up teaching, always believing that his footballing skills could be useful on the games field. Then his father died, although by that time Colin had already become a respected football coach with a particular empathy for the honest trier.

His first school was in one of the toughest areas of the county, where early on he decided he would get to know each child he taught individually. The reason was clear: he knew that many of those he taught were from tough backgrounds, just as he himself had experienced in his childhood; he regarded it as a privilege to be in a position where he could help these pupils 'make a real go of it' at his school.

By the time Colin had started at Graysfield, it was clear that this was an important aspect of his teaching. Children with little academic ability were incentivised by the prospect of an afternoon on the games field. So not only did they try harder in the classroom, they were less likely to cause trouble there or around the school – which, of course, made life much easier and more pleasant for everyone.

A key aspect of this strategy was that the teacher undertook to find out as much as he could about new pupils before they arrived at Graysfield. Of course, he would never let previous reputations obscure his judgment. As far as he was concerned, everyone started life at Graysfield with a blank canvas; it was then up to each one to show their true worth.

By now, the head of games had many friends in the teaching profession, and he particularly enjoyed meeting up with staff from the Graysfield 'feeder' schools for a coffee or a beer, when they would catch up on each other's news. It was rare for him to hear negative comments about his new pupils. Most of his teacher friends were positive thinkers who wanted the best for their pupils. Besides, Graysfield was an increasingly popular school, and so the children generally made sure they worked hard in order to secure a place there.

Many of the teachers Colin knew actually enjoyed telling him when their children were a delight to teach. And there were two words which were repeatedly used by his teachers to describe Jimmy Evans: "honest trier".

Colin liked these words. They actually meant more to him than "able pupil" or even "highly talented". He knew that an able or talented person would need to apply their talent in order to get on. Sometime, of course, this happened. But from experience, he knew it sometimes did not. *Besides,* reasoned the coach, *which student is more likely to listen: a talented individual who has often been told that they are talented or an honest trier who knows he needs help to improve?* He would do his best for every student in his care, but it was the honest trier he found he could most easily relate to and with whom, looking back, he reckoned he had had most success.

Jimmy knocked on Mr. Smith's door and, when invited, entered to face the head of games.

"Sit down, Jimmy. I understand from Miss Britton that you had a set-to with Bobby Ford this morning."

"Yes, sir," admitted Jimmy.

"I'd like you to tell me what happened, Jimmy. I understand Bobby was sent to First Aid."

So Jimmy told Mr. Smith the whole story.

"Let me get this straight. Are you saying you did not start the argument, Jimmy?"

"Yes, sir." Jimmy was tense and nervous as he waited for Mr. Smith's reply.

"You see, Jimmy, Miss Britton has gained the impression that you were to blame. You clearly think she is mistaken."

"Yes, sir."

"Was there anyone else around who might have seen it as it happened?"

"Only Kai Stevens, sir," replied Jimmy. "He was with Bobby."

The head of games raised his eyebrows in sudden interest. But he said nothing.

Suddenly Jimmy remembered Tommy Newton standing by the wall eating. "Oh," he added quickly, "Tommy was nearby, but I think he was more interested in his orange."

The head of games seemed to consider for a moment, then made an entry in his notebook.

"Thank you, Jimmy," he said. "That will be all for now. You may go."

"Thank you, sir," replied Jimmy, and he left the room. But he wondered, as he made his way back outside, whether he had in fact said enough to convince the coach that he was still a boy to be trusted.

———————————

Tommy Newton wondered why on earth he had been asked to see Smithy in his room.

Mr. Smith got straight to the point. "Did you see any incident between boys when you were outside in morning break, Tommy?"

"Yes, sir, I did," replied Tommy promptly. "You know Bobby Ford? 'e shouted out so loud all of a sudden – made me drop me orange. Jus' finished peelin' it too, sir – all in one go. An' then, oops – it's gone, right in the mud. I'm not fussy, sir, but I couldn't eat it after that, could I? Not covered in mud – no way!"

"Well, I'm sorry about your orange, Tommy," replied Mr. Smith sympathetically. "But can you tell me anything else about the incident?"

"Not really, sir. It were only when Bobby yelled that I realised 'e were there. I mean, he was on the other side of the yard before that, chattin' with Kai Stevens, by the basketball."

The head of games knew all of the boys. Tommy Newton was not a mixer. But he did notice what was going on around him as a rule.

"So, who else was involved, Tommy?" he pursued.

"Well, that were Jimmy Evans, sir. He were involved. But he'd not been out there long. I saw him coming out when I started peelin' me orange."

"So are you saying Jimmy had been in that area and nowhere else?" asked the coach.

"I'm sure he must 'ave, sir," replied Tommy frankly.

"Thanks, Tommy. You may go," said the head of games, and he promptly picked up his mobile phone.

16

KAI AT THE CROSSROADS

Mr. Watson was congratulating himself on a peaceful breaktime. Everything seemed in order, no scuffles. "Yes," he muttered to himself. "It's going well."

Just then his phone rang. It was Colin Smith, asking Watson if he would kindly send Kai Stevens to meet him in the sports hall. That was simple enough. Kai was just yards away, laughing and joking with Bobby Ford. Watson duly called Kai and passed on the message.

"Well done, Kai!" Bobby shouted after him as he left. "I bet that's to tell you you're in the team. Good one!"

Kai hurried eagerly to see the football coach.

"Kai," began Mr. Smith, "I'd like you to tell me about this morning's incident between Bobby Ford and Jimmy Evans, when Miss Britton tells me you took Bobby to First Aid."

"Well, yeah, sir, I 'ad to take Bobby to First Aid, sir – yeah, that's right, sir – 'cos of Jimmy. Yeah, sir, Jimmy hit him into the rose bushes, sir."

"So, why do you think he did that, Kai?" quizzed the teacher.

"Sorry, sir – what d'you mean, sir? Like I said, sir, 'e just did it. Yeah, knocked 'im in the bushes, sir, 'e did."

"Strange," commented Mr. Smith. "For no reason, Jimmy laid into Bobby?"

"Yes, sir," mumbled Kai.

"So he started a fight with Bobby, even though you were already with him? Because you *were* already with him, weren't you, Kai?"

Kai was confused. All that could come out now were 'um's and 'err's.

"Were you and Bobby not both over by the basketball pitch earlier in break, Kai?" the head of games asked persistently.

"Yes, sir," replied Kai, though not quite sure where this was leading.

"Miss Britton clearly told me the incident took place by the rose bushes, near the school entrance," Mr. Smith explained. "I am led to believe that Jimmy Evans had not moved further into the playground from that place – which seems to suggest that for some reason you and Bobby Ford decided to move away from the basketball pitch towards Jimmy."

Kai was tongue-tied. Snookered. A fair cop. He hung his head and said nothing.

The teacher looked at his watch. "Kai," he said firmly, "bad behaviour we can deal with. Everyone makes mistakes. But I must have the truth. And," he added, "the same applies in football too. In my team you don't have to be a superstar, but if you're an honest trier who gives me a hundred per cent, then I am interested."

Kai stood thoughtful. Smithy's words, though firm, appeared to be offering him a lifeline out of the mess he had got himself into.

"Let me put this to you, Kai," he continued. "I suggest you have two options. You can either continue the way you are, pushing yourself around as though you're the only one that matters, forget everyone else – or you can start to realise the fantastic opportunities you could have by applying yourself in the classroom, and trying to get on with others."

Kai pondered a moment. The way Smithy had put it, he could see two pathways ahead of him. And only one, he reckoned, made any sense. He then remembered the words of both his parents before he had started at Graysfield, only two weeks ago: "A fresh start, Kai. Just start again – and make it work." Their words touched something deep inside him. Yes, he had wanted to make a fresh start at Graysfield. He had been impressed by the lovely facilities and green spaces when he had visited with his primary school mates on Induction Day. He had looked forward to science and technology and art – and of course, games. But he had messed up – not made a good start. And he felt ashamed.

A tear came to his eye. He struggled to hold himself together. But he had decided. The coach's words, coupled with the remembered message from his doting parents, had been a breakthrough – a 'lightbulb moment', causing a change of heart. He would change his ways – or at least he would try. It would probably need effort – but it should be worth it.

And then – oh no! Not in front of the football coach… What could be worse? But the more he struggled to contain his feelings, the more he felt churned up inside. Suddenly, and partly to prevent himself blubbing in front of the teacher, he burst out, "We started it, sir, not Jimmy. Sir, I'm sorry. Really I am, sir—"

And yes, he burst into tears.

Colin Smith did not like to see Kai crying. He would never want that. But he reckoned it was a breakthrough, a turning point in 'the story of Kai'. *Now,* he reckoned, *here is someone I can work with, reason with, someone with whom I can connect – and hopefully help him achieve something, something of which he can be proud. There is surely no further need for punishment – through his realisation and remorse, Kai has probably gone through enough.*

But there were still ends to tie up. Jimmy needed to receive an apology. Bobby Ford needed to be dealt with. And everyone, not least those hoping to make it into the team, needed to see justice done.

17

A NEW FRIENDSHIP

Mr. Smith laid a compassionate hand on Kai's shoulder. "Kai," he said, in the kind yet firm and understanding way that the boys respected, "I can see you're sorry. I am sure now you want to make a fresh start to your life at Graysfield. And I shall try to help you do just that." He took another glance at his watch. "So here is your first challenge," he continued. "If you like, the first challenge in the life of the new Kai. Two things actually. Firstly, I want you to say something to Jimmy. I'm not going to tell you what to say – you can work that out. Secondly, you must make it clear to Bobby Ford that you are changing course; there must be no confusion about that. Kai, this is something you yourself must do, but I will do all I can where appropriate to help you make it work. Off you go – and give it your best shot."

Kai thanked the head of games as he left his room, and then headed straight outside, hoping to find Bobby. He did not have to wait long. Bobby had been lurking close to the entrance, eager to find out how his mate had got on with the coach. But he was totally unprepared for Kai's first words.

"Bobby," he said, "I'm gonna turn it round. What's the use of messing around all the time? It only gets you into trouble. In any case, I wanna make the team. Every way, I guess I gotta turn it round."

Jimmy and Kai shook hands, but immediately turned it into a high five.

Bobby was stunned. He opened his mouth, but nothing came out. Just then, Kai saw Jimmy across the yard. He moved over towards him.

"Jimmy," he called, "I'm sorry. I've bin stoopid. Just an idiot really. I'm gonna change. I'm really sorry for messin' you about."

He held out his hand. Jimmy, knowing that Kai had seen Smithy, was delighted, though not that surprised. By now he had grown to trust the games teacher as one who could sort things out – not dramatically, no, but effectively. He shook hands, but immediately turned it into a high five. This released something inside Kai, who laughed spontaneously.

Bobby Ford was watching on with interest. *Maybes I oughta start doin' some thinkin' meself...*

Smithy had come back outside, and had witnessed the making up between Kai and Jimmy. He would still need to show the rest of his football squad that bad behaviour did not pay though. He walked over to the two boys.

"I see you boys have made up," he said. "That's good. However, if you are to play in the school football team, you will both have a point to prove. And I'm not just talking skills."

The boys understood what Smithy was saying.

"Sir, I'll really do my best," responded Jimmy.

"Count me in on that," added Kai.

And the bell rang for afternoon classes, with both Jimmy and Kai secretly hoping that they might make it into the football team.

18

MATCH DAY

Kai was as good as his word. In fact, more than once Jimmy overheard a member of staff referring to him as "a changed person".

"Is it the same boy?" asked Miss Petty, not known for her compliments. "I just can't believe how his whole attitude has changed."

"Same lad, all right," affirmed Mr. Harris. "But I agree, there is a massive difference."

And so it was that the football coach was able to select both Kai *and* Jimmy for the match at St. Mary's the following week.

The day of the Big Match dawned bright and clear, and Jimmy was first into the bathroom that morning. After washing and dressing, he rushed downstairs and made sure all his kit was ready in his sports bag before hurrying into the kitchen for his breakfast. Cornflakes and milk, toast and marmalade and a glass of fresh orange juice set him up nicely for the exciting day ahead.

The school day seemed to pass so slowly – but at last it was time to leave for the match. The team were allowed to miss the final lesson of the day, so as to leave in time to get to St. Mary's for a four o'clock kick-off.

The boys piled into the minibus. Mr. Smith checked that everyone had fastened their seatbelts before he climbed into the driver's seat.

"Just a few tips to bear in mind before we start," he said.

The coach's planning and preparation were meticulous, so the boys listened intently.

"I am pretty sure their two strikers will be the ones they had when I saw them last. My nephew is in his school team, and they played St. Mary's recently. It was my half-day, so I went along to support him. The strikers were not bad, but when I saw them, there were points worth noting. The taller one is not keen on being tackled. So you, Johnny, make sure your tackling is clean and fair but hard – you'll probably be marking him. And you, Freddie, you'll probably be on the other boy. He's much shorter and more stocky. He has a good shot, but he lacks pace. You just make sure – with your pace – that you get there first every time! Otherwise, all of you, feel free to play your own best game. Enjoy seeing what you can do – but always playing as a team. Support each other. Go for it! I know I'm looking forward to it!"

Mr. Smith started the engine, and the team were on their way.

The coach had not yet told Kai and Jimmy which of them would start the match. This was deliberate. He knew of course that they had made up for the playground incident of the day before. Even so, he knew boys well enough to know that in a situation like this, where one would have to get the nod over the other, even after making friends there could be tension or resentment. He would tell them later, making sure the one missing out still had plenty to look forward to.

Mr. Smith started the engine, and the team were on their way.

As Mr. Smith drove into the car park, the St. Mary's games teacher came to greet them, with his team also on hand to welcome the boys. Greetings concluded, the teams trotted off to the match field.

As they approached the field, the coach called Kai and Jimmy.

"Kai," he said, "I'd like you to start the match. And I want you on the right wing. If you can get past your full-back, make sure you send over some good crosses for Noah and Abdul. Then it's up to them, isn't it?"

He gave a cheeky grin at Abdul, who was listening in.

"And tell Noah what I said, Abdul," he added.

Jimmy was a little disappointed at not starting – but not too much. He had known all along that the eleventh spot would go either to him or to Kai – and he might still go on later as sub anyway.

Mr. Smith interrupted Jimmy's thoughts.

"Jimmy," he said, "Kai is a shade more experienced than you, having played for his local team. So that's why I've put him on at the start. But I want you to watch their players carefully, so that if you go on, you know something about them which might help you."

Jimmy, on reflection, thought this was a good idea. He told the coach so, took a long swig from his drink bottle and determined to learn something of use from the opposition.

Then he put down his bottle and opened up his kit bag. He had just had an idea. Fairly obvious, really. He took out his notebook and pencil. He always took these two items with him when he went anywhere interesting – ever since receiving a merit certificate from his Year 4 class teacher for his description of 'My weekend visit to Wookey Hole'. Not only was the teacher pleased, but his classmates also had cooed and gasped at his vivid descriptions of caves, frozen lakes and stalagmites.

He would not just trust his thoughts and observations to memory; he would write them down. He waited eagerly for the referee to call the captains, positioning himself on the touchline in line with the centre-spot.

The referee, a short, stocky man in an Aston Villa shirt, got the game going. Graysfield kicked off and were soon on the attack. Noah shot wide and Abdul's close-range effort was blocked. Further attacks were mounted, but St. Mary's defence were holding out, their keeper making a string of good saves.

One of their defenders was a particularly athletic-looking boy, tall and broad-shouldered, who was controlling everything around him and allowing little past him. Jimmy opened his notebook and wrote:

Big, strong defender – try the wings.

The Graysfield forwards continued to attack, but were getting little joy until Charlie, playing a storming game in midfield, sent a long ball out to the right wing.

Jimmy was pleased to see that his team mates had similar thoughts to his own. Soon both wingers were more involved, and it seemed just a matter of time before a goal would come. Several attempts were snuffed out by the strong-tackling full-backs, before Kai managed to send over a cross which eluded everyone. Noah was about to pull the trigger when the St. Mary's keeper made a brave save to deny him.

The keeper punted a long ball forward. It bypassed the midfield and dropped, conveniently for St. Mary's, at the feet of their shorter striker, the one Mr. Smith had warned had a decent right foot. Freddie was right next to him, marking him closely. But the boy's first touch was outstanding. He brought the ball down and turned to face goal, setting it up before unleashing a strong right-footed drive which sped towards the Graysfield goal. Josh, in goal, saw it speeding towards him, but at the last moment the ball swerved ominously out of his reach and towards the top corner of the net. There was nothing he could do. It was a super strike. St. Mary's were in front, and Graysfield had it all to do.

Almost immediately, the whistle blew for half-time.

The teams trooped off the pitch to their respective coaches and slices of orange to restore energy levels. As usual, Mr. Smith looked relaxed and not too concerned.

"Boys, you're not playing badly," he began. "St. Mary's are a good team, and you're giving them a decent game."

"They've got some massive defenders, sir," exclaimed Noah.

"Yeah, job to get past their centre-back," added Abdul.

"You're right, boys," agreed the coach. "So there are one or two things we can try which might just help. I'm pleased to see you are beginning to get the ball out now to our wingers. That way you're stretching their defence; they'll need to cover more of the pitch. So keep that going. But also, if you can then run in behind the defence, you're forcing them to turn. Many defenders prefer to deal with the threat in front of them. They're usually not so keen when the attackers are getting in behind."

The boys appeared to have got the message, so the coach finished by saying, "Right, boys – let's see if we can turn this one around – and have fun!"

The boys ran off to resume their challenge.

19

JIMMY MAKES HIS MARK

Mr. Smith turned to Jimmy. "Well, Jimmy, I saw you making notes. What did you reckon?"

Jimmy showed his teacher the simple note he had written:

Big, strong defender – try the wings.

"That's good, Jimmy. Very observant. You might make a coach one day. But it's one thing to observe these things from the line; let's see if we can go out there and get it right."

They watched the match together. Graysfield had started the half on the attack, and clearly were trying to heed their coach's words. The ball was moving out to the wings more frequently now, with Kai on the right and Terry Baker on the left wing making good runs, but without yet being able to get in a telling cross. Indeed, neither winger had been able to get past their full-back, and so what crosses there had been were easily dealt with by the tall, athletic St. Mary's defenders. The coach could see that more pace was needed down the flanks to beat the full-back and send over a cross to trouble the compact St. Mary's defence. He knew Jimmy had pace. Could he make a difference? He might have the speed to beat his man, yes, but could he deliver a cross that might unlock this cool, stubborn defence? Jimmy had not shown consistency in that area yet. But if he could do it once, that might be enough...

The coach looked at his watch. Fifteen minutes to go. Realistically, now was the time to make a change so as to give a reasonable chance of a breakthrough.

"Jimmy," he said.

"Yes sir?"

"If you went on now, what would you be trying to do?"

"I'd try to beat the full-back and send over a cross for the strikers, sir," replied Jimmy without hesitation.

"And do you reckon you might just manage that?"

"I'd have a good go at it, sir."

"That's my boy. Take your top off."

Jimmy removed his tracksuit top and placed it in his kit bag.

"Just jog down to the corner flag and back," said the coach.

Jimmy carried out the routine and returned ready for action, then jogging briefly on the spot.

The ball was kicked out of play. Colin signalled to the referee that he would like to make a substitution. He had intended taking off Kai. However, Abdul was clearly tiring, having struggled manfully against strong opponents. Kai had played as striker before. He could replace Abdul, with Jimmy taking Kai's place on the wing.

The coach quickly told Jimmy the plan, and signalled to Abdul to come off. Abdul didn't seem too sorry, and made straight for his kit bag for a good, long swig of water.

"Good effort, Abdul," the coach encouraged with a smile. "Make sure you keep warm."

Jimmy ran across to take up position on the right wing.

Most of the play was still taking place in the St. Mary's half. The Graysfield defence had been largely untroubled since half-time, apart from another shot by their scorer which had been well saved by Josh, and a long-range effort from their other striker which had passed harmlessly wide of the post. The ball was at present on the Graysfield left, and moving forward. Terry was showing good control. He'd already managed to beat his man twice, sending over useful crosses to the forwards. The first had seen a very good effort from Noah sent just wide; the second saw Kai sending a low volley straight into the hands of the 'keeper. Terry was now jinking around his opponent, moving skilfully this way and that. Suddenly he found space by sprinting strongly past the full-back. Now he could cross. He sent over a perfect ball, low and invitingly into the path of the onrushing midfielder, Saed. Saed met the ball beautifully, directing it away from the keeper and towards the far corner. The keeper dived and touched the ball, but pace and direction beat him as the ball scorched into the net and nestled in the far corner. A great equalizer. Cheers all round. "Lovely cross, Terry!" "Well done, Saed – what a corker!"

One-all, with twelve minutes to go. Now, could the boys conjure up another goal, then hold on to win the match? Things were getting tense.

St. Mary's were right now making a rare foray into the Graysfield half. Freddie was doing a good job holding off the threat of the St. Mary's goal-scorer, while Johnny was ensuring the other striker was also kept quiet. Then, in a rare moment, St. Mary's right-winger, who previously had done little, found space to unleash a strong shot at the goal.

Josh, however, was ready for the threat, and positioned himself early enough to make a good diving save at the near post. He clutched the ball and looked up, considering whether to go left or right. He spotted Jimmy ready and waiting against the right-hand touchline, and sent a long punt in his direction. Jimmy watched as the ball sailed through the air over the midfield and down towards him, waiting expectantly on the wing. He had studied his opposing full-back carefully throughout the game and was confident that once he had the ball under control, he would have a fair chance of beating him. It would then be a matter of doing all he could to get a really good cross over to the strikers.

The ball dropped invitingly half a yard from him. His first touch was good, and although the full-back was right by him, he had the ball in his control. He paused, considering which way to get past the back. He nicked the ball outside of the boy and away from the defenders, though now he was quite close to the touchline. But he backed himself to avoid kicking it out for a throw-in. He flicked the ball on, just inside the line and far enough ahead to enable him to outrun his opponent. Then he collected the ball before it had run to the goal line, and looked quickly towards the strikers. Noah, the taller of the two, was by now ten yards from the far post – but was being closely marked by St. Mary's giant defender. Kai was more central, near the penalty spot and not quite so closely marked. Jimmy, eye now on the ball, made sure of a good contact which would lift the ball back into the penalty area, hopefully in such a way that Kai could meet it and score.

It was a good, firm connection. The ball rose from Jimmy's orange boot towards the centre of the penalty area, but tantalisingly moving away from the St. Mary's keeper. Had it been a yard or so closer, he would have had no trouble in moving out to claim the ball. But it was too far out for that, and moving away from him – far too risky to follow. If he were to miss the ball, as would then be likely, his goal would be at the mercy of the Graysfield strikers. The keeper stayed on his line, ready and hoping.

Kai was waiting. He guessed that Jimmy's cross would not be as strong as one of his own, but reckoned it could still be good enough to give him a chance of scoring. As it happened, he was surprised when Jimmy sent over the best cross Kai had ever seen from him, and it was close enough to reach easily.

Kai hardly had to move to receive the ball. He just needed to raise his foot and trap the ball, making sure it was a good contact. The ball now at his feet, he looked up to check his options. His split-second mind-training told him that the far side of the keeper was not a good option; 'tall boy' was lurking around, together with two other defenders. But there was a small gap between the keeper and his near post. If he kept the ball down, it could be difficult for the keeper to get down in time to make a save. Kai had as good an eye as anyone. He always won prizes at the shooting range when the travelling fair arrived, and he was a dab hand at darts. But his footwork was good too. He eyed the gap and took careful aim.

It was one of those golden moments when, as a striker, you know as soon as you have struck the ball that it's a goal. Even Mr. Smith gave a cheer!

The boys were ecstatic. But there were still several minutes to go – as the coach now called to remind them. "All hands to the pump. Don't let them back in now, boys!"

If anything, the boys, who had been working hard throughout the match – their shirts were evidence of that – now found yet another gear. Every fifty-fifty ball was won or quickly won back, and Graysfield found themselves dominating play in their opponents' half.

In the last minute there was even a chance for 3-1, when Jimmy found himself almost in a position to shoot. But he was quickly dispossessed by a defender. Shortly after, the referee put the whistle to his mouth and blew for full-time.

Sweet victory!

20

HUNGRY FOR MORE

Jimmy loved bangers, beans and chips. And I tell you, never had so scrumptious a meal tasted better than it did following that famous victory. Not only had he got on to play, he had actually supplied the cross for the winning goal – and that, after the team had been a goal down. Everyone was bubbling. Even the coach was beaming.

The slap-up meal was unusual; St. Mary's were, as far as the boys knew, the only school that provided more than a cup of squash and a biscuit or three following a match. Apparently one of the St. Mary's team's mums was actually the school caterer, and as well as being an excellent cook, she also had a big heart. She had no problem in summoning her team of friends to help provide the post-match meals, and it was the same team, together with other parents and friends, who organised a programme of fundraising events at the school, the proceeds of which actually funded much more than match teas. Over the years the 'mums' team' had provided funding for new football kits for the team, books for the school library, computers for the IT room and even fresh equipment for the school's well-used kitchens. No wonder St. Mary's was a happy school. As headmaster, Simon Rowson proudly admitted, "A happy school is often a successful school." Clearly everyone agreed.

But there was more to come. No sooner had they polished off the bangers, beans and chips, than the boys received another treat, as 'Cook' came round with a trolley laden with dessert dishes and three choices of ice cream – vanilla, strawberry and chocolate – for them to tuck in to. The boys were in heaven, especially as there was what seemed like an endless supply of orange squash or water to wash it all down. What a day !

At last the feast was over, and the coach summoned his bloated heroes to thank their hosts and leave for the car park.

"Sir, I reckon this has been one of the best days of my life," enthused Jimmy, as he returned with coach and mates to the minibus.

"And I'd go along with that!" called Kai, overhearing his team mate's comments.

That'll do for me, Colin thought, as he remotely unlocked the minibus in preparation for the return journey.

"Boys, you did yourselves proud," exclaimed the coach, as the boys climbed back into the minibus. "A fine performance indeed. And I've something else to tell you."

The boys were tired, but keen to listen.

"St. Mary's have a team of parents who raise money for the school through fairs and coffee mornings and the like. I've been thinking, wouldn't it be great if we could start something like that at Graysfield? I am sure there are plenty of things we could think of to raise money for."

"We could do with some more computers, sir," suggested Freddie.

"Yes – and a set of drums for our concerts," piped up Chris, who was crazy on drums, and whose older brother was trying to start up a group of his own.

"And sir, what about us getting an Astroturf pitch at our school?" contributed Noah, who played on Astro with his local under-twelves team.

"Ah, we can dream!" responded the coach. "But boys, remember, there are some children, even some schools, that don't even have a football pitch at all. So maybe we should consider the difference between what we would like to have and what we really need."

The boys fell quiet for a moment. The point had been made. But the teacher did not want them to remain sombre.

"Yes, there's plenty we can do if we work together, boys," he rejoined enthusiastically. "And boys, you certainly have shown that today!"

He started the engine, and the minibus eased its way out of the car park.

21

MASTER PLAN

The match at St. Mary's, together with the superb after-match meal, had been an occasion to remember, and it dominated many conversations among those involved for days to come. But strangely it was the conversation in the minibus prior to the journey back to school which had remained with some of the team. Some of the coach's words had struck home: "Boys, there are some children, even some schools, that don't have a football pitch at all."

Jimmy, for one, was fully aware of this. Had he not chosen Graysfield because of its football facilities? So he was certainly keen to continue the fundraising conversation with the coach whenever the occasion might arise. Smithy, too, had been thinking about the conversation in the bus, as became evident at their next after-school practice.

The head of games greeted the boys briefly, and soon had them warming up by jogging up and down the pitch from goal to centre line and back several times. He then set about his well-planned and rehearsed warm-up exercises, from stretches and running on the spot to squat thrusts, 'cycling' and press-ups. He quickly progressed to 'challenges' in pairs and fours, after which the cones were used – first for in-and-out sprinting, then for dribbling and close ball control. Then, having organised four small teams, he would have two short games, side by side.

And here, right on cue, was the new coach.

"Hi, Martin!" Smithy called. "I've split the boys into four teams, two 'A's and two 'B's. I'll take the 'A's over here, if you'd kindly take the 'B's over there. We'll give them twenty minutes each way, and you and I can swap over at half-time. Let me know if you unearth any gems – though, realistically, your boys will probably need plenty of encouragement more than anything else. And don't forget – they all want to make it one day!"

Twenty minutes later, the head of games blew his whistle, and everyone assembled in the main goalmouth for drinks and a half-time debriefing.

"Well, Martin, have you found any stars?" Colin asked his assistant.

"Everyone's got stuck in," replied Martin. "But Tommy Newton really impressed me today."

"Tommy, eh? Good lad," Smithy applauded. "And I'm glad to hear everyone's had a go," he continued, "because I've been having a few thoughts."

He turned to the 'A' squad.

"Lads," he said, "do you remember what we were discussing after the match the other day?"

"Sir, you were saying how lucky we were to have a football pitch," Jimmy replied.

"That's right, Jimmy. And is there anything else we might feel lucky about?"

"It felt really good to be included in the team," spoke up Kai. Some of the others in the team nodded in agreement.

"That's nice of you to say that, Kai," said their coach. "You see, you can't put twenty-four boys into one football team, can you?"

There was tacit agreement. Smithy looked over towards the 'B' group.

"I was talking with the St. Mary's coach the other day, boys," he said. "He tells me he has many boys who can't get into the first team that he would like to play in a game. And he asked me if I could get up a second team."

It was as if an electric forcefield had suddenly struck the ground where the 'B' team were sitting. Everyone looked at the coach.

"And... and what did you say, sir?" asked Bill Bradbury, a faithful regular.

"I said I'd definitely give it some thought. There would be one or two matters to sort out first."

"What are those, sir?" This time it was voices from both squads who were asking the question.

"Well, boys, I reckon you can work it out for yourselves," replied Mr. Smith. "I mean, what do you need in order to put on a football match?"

"A pitch."

"A football."

"Players, teams."

"A ref."

"Yes, I think we can provide all of those in this school, don't you? Anything else?"

The boys thought for a moment. Then one piped up, "Sir, all those who are playing would need to be wearing their team's kit."

"You're right," replied the coach. "And just let's think what items go into a football kit."

Within seconds "shirt", "shorts" and "socks" were all called out. Someone added "tracksuit". And "boots", suggested another.

Jimmy looked down with pleasure at his orange boots – well, *brown* and orange at the moment. He picked some clods of mud from between the studs.

"Yes – boots," Smithy confirmed. "Really, those are your 'tools of the trade', as you may say. They enable you to play your best game. Look after them. Try to keep them nice and supple, so that your toes and feet can work comfortably inside them. After matches and practices, try to get all the mud off and then get them nice and clean with a damp rag. When they're dry, there are all sorts of conditioners you can buy from sports shops to keep them in top nick. So yes, take care of your boots."

Colin looked round at the boys sitting on the ground before him. Kit-wise, at least, they were quite a motley array, really. A fair number, mainly in the 'A' game, were wearing full kit, with shorts, socks and a football shirt. Some Rovers, some City, some Liverpool or Chelsea. A fair number, mainly in the 'B' game, were wearing T-shirts; one or two had open-neck shirts which had probably been worn to school that day.

"How many of you would like to play in a match if you were given the opportunity?" he enquired.

Every hand shot up.

That's it, Colin thought to himself. *We need another set of kits – and that means money!*

"Right, boys," he said. "Thanks for your ideas. I must put my thinking cap on. Meanwhile, let's continue our games."

Smithy moved over to the 'B' players' pitch, allowing Martin to take charge of the 'A' squad. In no time at all the field was humming with the efforts of boys of varying abilities – and the head of games detected an extra energy in the 'B' game, as compared to previous weeks.

Colin had made up his mind to form a second team. The St. Mary's coach had already agreed to play home and away matches between the schools if Graysfield could raise two teams. But new kits required money – and where was that to come from? For years now, budgets had been tight, with any money needed for extracurricular activities needing donations or fundraising events to do the business.

He glanced around the sports hall. His eyes rested on a corner of the hall where Mr. Harris had posted a display of Year 9 art work – 'Portraits of Each Other'. The previous display had been 'Still Life', and before that, some quite impressive paintings entitled 'Views from Our School'.

In addition to his displays of children's paintings, Mr. Harris also regularly had his students producing some quite acceptable clay items – jugs, plates and pots – which were always attractively displayed.

Then there were the 'Design and Technology' and Textiles departments, each of which managed to produce surprisingly impressive items even on a restricted budget. The staff in these departments were enterprising, energetic and enthusiastic – three qualities which Colin felt might be invaluable in any joint effort or project such as might include an exhibition or display. Colin knew there would be plenty of other offers to help inside, including music and the performing arts in the Main Hall, should he suggest a major fundraising event for the school.

On top of all that he was confident of arranging a full, challenging programme of events on the school fields.

Of course, visitors would need refreshments. The dining room would be available for light meals and snacks, and outside areas for a barbecue. Colin was confident he could get plenty of volunteers to organise both.

The head of games slipped back into his office and jotted down ideas into his multi-purpose notebook. Every idea recorded produced a satisfied glow of anticipation in the mind of the experienced coach, until he became more and more convinced he was really on to something.

And the name of the event? considered the coach, as he concluded his notes. *Of course... 'Graysfield's Got Talent'.*

22

Spreading the Word

Colin Smith decided to bring up his plan with the headmaster and, if he was willing, to present his ideas in a staff meeting so that everyone would know what was going on. Steve Smart was a positive, approachable head who actually loved initiatives from his staff, especially when they were practical. When the head of games phoned him, he instantly gave his backing and agreed that Colin should raise the matter at next Tuesday's staff meeting.

––––––––––––

The response was even better than Colin could have imagined. Everyone agreed that the event should go ahead, and many were confident that their present projects were likely to produce a reasonable number of results. The head of home economics, who happened to be on the Parent-Teacher Association, volunteered to set up a team to produce stalls for cakes, biscuits etc. at the very least.

The main school hall, used daily for lunches, would, it was generally agreed, be the best area for visitors to sit for lunches or snacks, while the barbecues – yes, there was general agreement there could and should be *two* – could take place on the forecourts outside the school buildings.

The art and craft teachers were particularly energised, and suggested that their students would be encouraged to produce items for display – "Yes, more work for the art staff, but what's new!" In addition, really keen or outstanding contributors could also command a place at a table in the sports hall, an area large enough, surely, for everyone who might wish to do extra. There they would display their handiwork, and invite visitors to contribute to the overall fund with a donation at the door.

By now everyone was bubbling. In fact it was a job for the head now to regain everybody's attention, so fervent were the ideas being suggested. Miss Jones, head of music, was very keen that the performing arts should take part. She realised, of course, that it would be difficult to hold anything like a concert while so many were involved in other activities. Colin was ready for this, and assured Miss Jones that there was no way the performing arts would have anything but a major part to play in 'Graysfield's Got Talent'. No, it wouldn't be possible to have a concert on that day; however, he believed it would be possible, were the music staff kindly to agree, to have timed sessions in the main school hall, where students could perform for a short time. They would be selected on the basis of those who were willing to contribute towards the day. Hopefully, at some later stage, some of those who had performed might be asked to perform in a school concert.

Colin thanked everyone profusely, before outlining the activities he envisaged for the school fields. The idea would be that as many as possible would be sponsored – preferably by the individual competitor's friends and family, meaning that there would be a good chance that they would pay up on the day. *Sooner in, the better,* he always thought. *Get it banked, get it done.* Each competitor would be encouraged to either run, jog or walk around the marked track a chosen number of times. There would be a team of organisers and checkers, hopefully taken from the sixth form and school prefects, who would man tables at different points around the field; each competitor would have submitted a form indicating precisely what they planned to do on the day. There would also be six-a-side football and netball, by year groups, for those unable to obtain sponsor money. Those taking part would be encouraged to contribute whatever they could to the whole school effort. Pretty well something for everyone, you could say.

The headmaster phoned the head of games early on Thursday morning.

"I'm proposing we hold a full school assembly to-morrow," he said. "I shall say a few words, and would then be grateful if you would outline your plans to the school. Time is short. We must kindle an interest which hopefully can spread full-on to families and community."

Colin was more than up for it. He offered there and then to draft a programme which he would run past the head later that day, prior to circulating to everyone the following day, giving them a chance to make inroads with family and community over the weekend.

Everyone knew the drill for 'full school assembly'. At 11.00 a.m. all KS3 years gathered in the large sports hall, ready for special info / announcements. Items were kept brief, so that hopefully by 11.20, KS3 would depart, allowing for KS4 and the sixth form to attend at 11.30. It invariably worked as the best way of conveying info urgently and quickly, face-to-face.

Accordingly, after morning break on Friday everyone gathered in the main hall for full school assembly. The staff guessed it related to last Tuesday's meeting but had 'kept mum' to the pupils. The children's guesses ranged from 'extra holiday' to 'school inspection'; they just didn't know.

The headmaster kept his words to a minimum – just enough to show that he and the staff were giving full support to what Mr. Smith was about to come up with. When the head mentioned the head of games, some Year 7 footballers did wonder whether there would be mention of some of the ideas they had had recently; but no one could possibly have been prepared for what Mr. Smith was about to present to the school that morning.

"I don't mind saying," he began, "that this is the best school I've ever worked in – and I have a shrewd suspicion that many here would feel the same. And it's because we're such a good school that we're always looking to provide the best for our students. As you know, education budgets are tight these days, so anything extra normally depends on fundraising, and that largely relies on the goodwill of as many as possible who have the school's interests at heart.

"Let's come to the point. Not everyone is an Albert Einstein, though we do expect you to do your best in the classroom. But that's one reason why we have extra-curricular activities such as games, so that after your daily slog you can let rip out there. We want as many of you as possible to enjoy our games facilities – and, given the chance, to represent a school you are proud of. But of course, teams need kit, and kits need money.

"But it's not just netball and football. Computers and books, though adequately resourced here at present, are areas where we could expand and improve. In fact, anything we can do to improve your experience here – and you all know how important school is for life, I'm sure – we will try to do.

"Now there's an urgency here. We have shedloads of children desperate to play – but we have insufficient kits. And the seasons are progressing fast. Wouldn't it be great if we could raise enough money to solve some of these issues by the October holiday? Yes, I know that's just four weeks from today. But fortunately the headmaster has checked with all staff and it is perfectly feasible to hold a major event here at Graysfield on Saturday 15th October, the last weekend before we break up. This will be big – big enough for every single one of us, hopefully supported by family and friends, to take part and make a contribution. And as we know you will all want to show us what you can do, it's obvious what we will call it: 'Graysfield's Got Talent'."

There was a wide buzz of excitement.

"Oh yes," continued Mr. Smith, with a twinkle in his eye, "I've little doubt there'll be one or two teenage heart-throbs strutting their stuff on the stage – to say nothing of other vocals and instrumentals, classic, jazz, rap and pop. Then there's art and craft of all types, science and technology – and of course sport. Then visitors will always need food. There will be something for everyone, and so much you can do. And you will receive a programme today outlining the timetable of events. So – that's the buzz! Now it's up to you, all one thousand and twenty of you, to convey that buzz to your families and friends, starting today. Just think what we can do if every one of us pulls out all the stops. I know you can do it. So – let's all do it for Graysfield!"

The head of games concluded with a brief, "Thank you, headmaster," and then returned to the side of the hall. In less than four minutes, he had got his message across to the school. Details would come later – but the seed had been sown.

23

ALL SYSTEMS GO

Over the next few days the school was more than ever a hive of activity. Most of Graysfield's students did apply themselves well to their studies – although there were always a stubborn few who were harder to persuade. But Smithy was a widely respected member of staff, and what he had said in the hall that Friday morning had affected even the toughest of customers.

Above all, it was a challenge – and an exciting one. And believe me, it was hard to find a single individual who did not wish to contribute to Graysfield's special day. Even Bill Langley, Year 9's Mr. Awkward, and hardly known for his positive comments, remarked, "I've never 'eard no one talk like that. Makes yer think."

The music staff quickly sounded out volunteers for the proposed 'recitals', gently reminding everyone that a donation or sponsorship would be a fair exchange for being selected to perform on the day. But it seemed as though no one needed reminding. Just about everyone was only too pleased to help in raising as high a total as possible. After all, if the school benefited then so, to an extent, did everyone.

As for the art department, the present displays were either added to or refreshed, giving constant reminders to all of the 'Big Event' to come.

Not that they were needed. A group of Year 8 boys decided they would love to organise side stalls for siblings. If siblings knew there would be side stalls, they would almost certainly want to come along, and if they came, their parents would come too. Hundreds of families coming along could make a massive difference.

So the Year 8s, aided by the head of design and technology, Mr. Bridge, soon compiled a wide array of attractions appealing to children, including hoopla, treasure maps, 'Guess the Teddy's Birthday', 'How Many Sweets in a Jar?' and mini skittles.

Meanwhile, Charley Simmons, a popular Year 8 girl, set up a group to organise a lucky dip. Her father, a local tradesman, had close dealings with wholesalers and very generously forwarded the money to obtain a thousand items at around 50p each on sale or return, such as would appeal to younger children. Charley and her friends then wrapped all the items within a week, ready for the big event.

And they simply couldn't wait.

———————————

It was the morning of the big event. Scheduled to open at ten and to run until four, phalanxes of mini scouts were to be seen peering in through the school gates from well before nine, eager to sample every shred of fun-time from this long-awaited day. Three weeks, after all, had been an age for an eight-year-old. Of course, they were not the first to arrive. By no means. The head of games had been stirring his coffee and checking his master plan shortly after seven, well in preparation for the arrival of his 'setting-up' team at eight. All the tables and chairs had been set out in the sports hall and dining hall overnight, with an adequate number also in the main hall, ready for the performing arts students and their supporters.

Colin felt somewhat like he usually did on a big match day: excited, slightly on edge, plenty of adrenaline. *But,* he thought, *this could top them all;* as far as he could tell, almost all the student population and well over ninety percent of staff were involved and committed. There were always staff for whom Saturday was the day when they visited a sick parent or something similar. But overall it had been a magnificent response.

Each area of the event would be well-organised and under the supervision of a designated team of leaders. The main hall would be controlled by the music staff, who had allocated hour-long slots for each year. The sports hall, with its art and craft exhibitions and display tables, had much longer time slots, with Years 7 to 9 exhibiting from ten to twelve, and Years 10 and above taking over the tables between one and three.

Outside, the field activities had, like the performing arts, been divided into hour-long slots. Since many had wished to contribute both indoors and out, slots had been staggered, with performing arts starting with the Year 9s. The field activities, involving the larger percentage of contributors, began at ten with Year 7s, running through to Year 11s between two and three. A chosen team of sixth formers were scheduled to help with checking and supervisory duties throughout the day; many of them were being sponsored by family for that, but some still wished to circuit the field and so there was a small team of staff who would be on hand at three to check their performance before signing their sponsor forms.

Many students had opted for six-a-side football or netball, with two adjacent games of each per hour. That way, with 'rolling subs', practically one third of the year intake could be accommodated this way. Smithy and Helen Hall, head of girls' games, had both recruited strong teams of helpers to cover the games for the day. They would run from shortly after the hour until twenty to, leaving twenty minutes for staff to recuperate!

The Year 8s had done a great job in preparing the sideshows – and Smithy had told them so. But he knew also that young, primary-aged visitors would need to let off steam at some time during the day. For this reason he had asked a group of sixth formers to supervise a play area for the younger visitors on one of the school fields, particularly focussing on the later stages of the day when the youngsters had run out of money.

Yes, thought Colin, *this should work.* He made a quick note, finished his coffee and closed his eyes, hoping to get a short nap before the big day ahead.

———————————

From just before eight, staff began to arrive. There was little to do, since most areas had been prepared the day before. But it was reassuring to see colleagues arriving and gradually moving to their areas for the day. There was a pleasant buzz as everyone prepared for the big event.

Well before nine o'clock, sixth formers arrived in droves and reported to Smithy. Shortly after, art and craft students made their way to the sports hall where they would set up their displays on their allocated tables. Eighty tables had been fitted into the large hall, most accommodating at least two pupils' work, meaning that almost one hundred and fifty of Years 7 to 9 in the morning and a similar number of Years 10 and above in the afternoon were afforded an exhibition space.

Two teams of barbecue cooks arrived in small vans and made their way purposefully to their designated pitches, one just around the corner from the main school entrance, the other a tarmacked area closer to the field.

All this time, sixth formers and prefects were helping out, some carrying tables and chairs pre-stored in an outbuilding on to the field, others to help with stewarding and supervision elsewhere.

At ten to ten, a team of school staff seated themselves at tables close to the school entrance. Admission was free, partly to speed up entry but also since most felt that people would then be more likely to give generously throughout the day.

But those who came did not enter empty-handed. Two thousand programmes were on hand, one for each family attending. The event had been well publicised locally, and so visiting families were certainly expected.

For Jimmy, who woke early that morning, this was the big day, and he was determined to make the most of every minute.

24

DRAMA ON THE 9.08

Jimmy had arranged to meet Luke and Brendan on the games field, after they had changed into their sports gear, ready for their sponsored jog or run together. It was a 'first' for all three, so they were not sure how many laps they would complete – or at what speed. One lap of the field was estimated to be four hundred metres, so they would put themselves down for ten laps. But secretly they were hoping and intending to do more.

Jimmy quickly changed into his games kit, before starting to fill his sports bag. He hurried downstairs and greeted Mum, who was already preparing in the kitchen.

"Morning, Jimmy! I know you'll probably buy burgers and whatnot at the school, but I've done you a packed lunch as well. Who knows – when you've done all that running, you'll probably be quite peckish and there could well be long queues. I know what you're like."

Mum thought of everything.

"Ah, thanks, Mum!" Jimmy beamed gratefully.

"There's a couple of bottles of squash and one of water. You'll need plenty of drinks to keep you hydrated."

He added the food and drinks to his sports bag before sitting down to his cereal.

"Well, all the best, Jimmy," called Mum, as he zipped up his bag and made for the door. "Here's your sponsor form."

Jimmy looked at the form and was delighted to see that Mum and Dad had each sponsored him for a pound a lap – and Uncle Reg two pounds for every lap of the field.

"That's brilliant, Mum – that means forty pounds if I do ten laps!" cheered Jimmy. "I reckon I will!"

And with that he put the form in his bag, gave Mum a hug and dashed off for the bus.

Jimmy had allowed plenty of time, since his bus ran only every forty minutes before ten on Saturday. The Year 7s had been told to arrive between 9.45 and 10.00 for the field activities. It would take Jimmy five minutes to walk from the bus to school, so he had planned to catch the 9.08, which should arrive at 9.38. There was little traffic around on Saturday morning, so the bus was usually on time. After a five minute wait, and very close to schedule, Jimmy's bus arrived. He stepped on the bus, showed his ticket and made his way inside.

Jimmy was about to go upstairs when he was surprised and delighted to see his a familiar face sitting halfway back in a window seat. It was his old lady friend. *How thoughtful of her!* he thought. The old lady had said she would like to support him, but he had really thought it might be a little too early in the day for her. Clearly, she had proved him wrong.

He moved towards her seat and raised his hand.

"Hello!" he greeted, with a smile. "How good to see you! Thanks so much for coming."

The old lady made no reply.

Jimmy looked closer. Her eyes appeared glazed. She seemed to be looking straight ahead and barely moving. It was clear to Jimmy that something was up. He glanced around the bus. The only other passengers on the lower deck were an elderly gentleman, who was fast asleep with his mouth wide open in one of the front side seats, and a couple of teenage boys, who appeared to be so engrossed in their iPad that it would take an age to alert them to anything else.

By now the bus had moved away from Jimmy's stop and was travelling at fair speed through his estate. Jimmy decided the old lady was sufficiently unresponsive to suggest she needed assistance. He must alert the driver. But he knew it was unwise to do so while the bus was moving. He looked ahead to see if anyone was waiting at the next stop. Good – there was a young lady with a small child waiting at the bus stop. Jimmy moved closer to the driver. As the bus drew up at the stop, he took the plunge.

"Excuse me," he said, "there is an old lady on the bus who appears to be unwell. I know her but she didn't recognise me when I spoke to her."

The driver, a young, alert-looking man with an open, friendly face, immediately switched off the engine, asked the young woman with toddler to "kindly wait a mo'" and strode back to the old lady.

"Hello," he said to her. "Can you hear me?"

No response.

He took a closer look. "You were right to tell me," he said to Jimmy. "Looks like she needs help." With that he took out his mobile phone and contacted his depot. "I've got an elderly passenger here," he said, "who I reckon needs medical help. Could you get me a paramedic? I'll wait here until they arrive."

It seemed the call was successful. The driver told the passengers and the woman and child combo that the bus would be stationary "for some time". The first announcement produced no response, so he went up to the teenagers, told them the situation, and they eventually moved slowly off the bus. As for the old gentleman, the driver needed to tap him gently on the shoulder to bring him back to earth.

Jimmy knew Luke and Bren would be expecting him soon. But he could not leave the old lady. He would be all the time wondering how she was. Jimmy picked up his mobile. He dialled Luke's number. No response. He tried Brendan. Again, no answer. He would try again later. He sat down and waited.

Jimmy glanced towards the old lady. She remained in the same position, pale and looking steadily ahead. The driver was standing beside her, checking his mobile. Jimmy thought of taking out his iPad – but no, he would have no heart to focus on anything else at the moment. He tried Luke again, then Brendan, each with the same result as before. Probably their phones were in their bags, and so they were not picking up. He sat back again and waited.

He looked out of the bus. Not much going on yet. Half-past nine. Few shops in this area, so not much activity. One or two cars and a cyclist passed. Otherwise, fairly quiet. Things would be starting up at school. Jimmy would have loved to have been there at the start, contributing, soaking up the atmosphere. He knew he would miss all that. He would be late. Luke and Bren would probably set off round the track without him. It would have been fun doing it together, maybe being cheered on by others. But no. This was where he should be. The old lady had clearly been on her way to support him. He could not possibly leave her without knowing she was OK. He waited.

Then he heard a siren. Faint at first, then gradually rising, clearly getting closer. He looked out of the front window of the bus and saw an ambulance hurrying along about three hundred metres away. Soon the ambulance had parked in front of the bus, sirens having stopped but blue lights still flashing, as a pair of paramedics – a burly red-faced man and a younger, petite female – boarded the bus. They made straight for the old lady, briefly pausing to exchange words with the driver.

"Do you know this passenger?" asked the burly man.

"Never seen her before," replied the driver, "but I am new to this route." And then, almost as an afterthought, he added, "I believe this young man here knows her."

The burly paramedic turned to Jimmy.

"So you know the old lady, eh? Would you be able to tell me if she normally enjoys good health?"

"Yes, as far as I know," replied Jimmy. Then he remembered a brief conversation he had had with her on a bus ride one day. "I believe she is diabetic," recalled Jimmy. "She takes insulin."

"Ah, now, that's helpful," replied the paramedic. "Any idea where she lives?"

"She told me she lives in Norton Street," answered Jimmy promptly, "and I think she said she goes to the same medical centre as my family at Broadley Walk."

"Why, you're a mine of information," continued the burly man. "Thanks!" He tapped a phone number on his mobile. "Hello, Broadley? Mark here. Got an elderly patient of yours by the name Mary Treasure. Need to know her insulin prescription – she's very poorly, and we need to give her something before moving her to the van."

Moments later, having received the information he needed, he spoke to his assistant, who quickly darted back to the ambulance, returning shortly after with a medical pouch, which she opened before quickly applying medication to the old lady's arm.

The paramedics looked on anxiously. A short pause, then the old lady's eyes began to flicker. Then her head slowly turned. She looked at the paramedics and tried to speak.

"Hi, Mary! You're on the bus and you've had a bit of a turn. Here, have a sip of this." The young paramedic helped the old lady to sip cool, clear water.

Gradually the old lady came round. "My, what time is it? I'm supposed to be—" Then she spotted Jimmy, sitting anxiously looking on. "Jimmy!" she gasped.

"Hi!" said Jimmy. "I hope you're feeling a little better."

"I think it's best if you come with us for a check-up," suggested the burly man. "Just to check you out, to be on the safe side."

The old lady was clearly distraught. "But I'm going to support Jimmy in his race at school," she protested.

Jimmy spoke up. "Mary, thank you," he said, "but I guess you should get better first. Tell you what, when we have another big event, I'll let you know straightaway."

The old lady opened her mouth as if trying to protest. But she didn't really have the energy. So she just quietly murmured, "Right, Jimmy," and closed her eyes.

The paramedics gently lowered her on to the roll-up stretcher they had brought on to the bus, and carried her to the waiting ambulance.

Once the paramedics had left with Mary, the bus driver explained that he needed to return to the depot, but he thanked Jimmy and wished him all the best for his big event.

Jimmy got off the bus and waited for the next one to arrive.

The 9.50 arrived within a minute of schedule. Jimmy calculated that it should arrive at his exit stop at around 10.20, meaning he would be 25 minutes later than he was expected at school. He tried again to phone his mates. Once more, no answer. They could be queuing to sign in. Or in

"I think it's best if you come with us for a check-up," suggested the burly man.

the changing rooms. Or just lapping up the fun. Whatever, they were not answering. He settled down to enjoy the near half-hour ride to school.

But he could not help thinking of other things. He was sure the old lady would be okay; she was in the hands of experienced paramedics. Jimmy was sure she would recover. But he wondered how he would get on at school, arriving so late for his run. *Oh well,* he thought, *no use worrying. Can't do anything about it.* Anyway, he was sure Smithy would understand when he told him his reason for being late.

His calculations, however, were way out. Because the earlier bus had been taken out of service, long queues had built up around Bentley and Dean Common. Jimmy reckoned they were getting later and later. It was nearly twenty past ten by the time they reached Archcombe Lane, and there were still half a dozen stops to go. Eventually, just after half-past-ten, the bus arrived at Jimmy's stop. He got off the bus and started running, but soon realised he ought to save his energy for the important running that lay ahead.

It was almost twenty to eleven by the time he made it to the games field. Would he be told off for being late? Had he missed his race slot? Jimmy just hoped his explanation, strange though it was, would be understood and accepted by those in charge.

Oh well, he thought, as he stepped on to the field. *Here goes!*

"Welcome to Graysfield, and thanks for coming!" the headmaster called.

25

A Day to Remember

By two minutes to ten a queue had already formed outside the main doors, which trailed across much of the area between the doors and main school gates. It was at this moment that the headmaster, smartly dressed as usual, and at his jovial best, emerged with a loudspeaker to briefly address the expectant crowd.

"Welcome to Graysfield, and thanks for coming!" he called. "We trust you will have a day to remember, and will be able to say you did your bit for 'Graysfield's Got Talent'. Enjoy your day!"

And with that, he signalled for the doors to be opened and for the big day to begin.

From that moment on it was 'all systems go', as key areas of the school filled with visitors who were all eager to be part of a special day. Certainly, this had been anticipated as a day to remember. Yet not even the most ardent supporter or the most cheerful optimist could have anticipated what was to be witnessed at Graysfield School that unforgettable day.

I invite you to imagine you are a local reporter using a zoom lens to take photographs, but also able to take snapshots from above with a drone. We enter the school, which is buzzing with excitement. We are soon in the main hall, and are immediately captivated by the enthusiasm of the performing pupils. On the stage at present is Sally Shepherd, doing her level best on the violin. Yes, you have heard better, but I challenge anyone to deny that Sally is putting every ounce of effort into her performance. And as she finishes her number, one is struck by the encouraging applause from the parents and other performers gathered in the hall.

We move on into the sports hall, where Mr. Harris and his team have in a short time produced magnificent art displays for the walls. They represent every school year and include school portraits, still life, scenes from the school, African sunsets and pop art. Staff near the door are already receiving generous donations and congratulations from the visitors. But the art displays are not all. The tables, manned by students, are laid out with all sorts of creative models and displays. The steam-engine corner, entertaining a bevy of interested admirers, is by no means the only attraction. A lengthy section of tables on one side of the hall displays a wide selection of motorised models likely to be the envy of any child with interest in toy or model aircraft, sports cars or three-wheelers.

On now into the dining hall. Yes, I could do with a coffee! But what is that delightful aroma tantalising my sensitive nostrils? We don't have to wait long for an answer. A clutch of twelve-year-olds appear, tucking into bags of cheese twists, freshly baked in the school kitchen. Must have some of that! We enter the hall and are impressed by the well-spaced tables already welcoming hungry, eager visitors preparing for a fun day out. There is a small queue at the serving hatch, but either side we notice large, colourful menus posted, inviting our custom. Soups, salads and simple meals including bangers-and-mash are all available, as well as crisps, pasties – and, of course, freshly baked cheese twists. But first things first. Tea or coffee are available for a pound while fizzy drinks cost something similar, and squash can be bought for 50p. Everyone seems happy, as they keenly examine their programmes and plan their itinerary for the day.

Refreshed and expectant, we move on to see, out of sheer curiosity, how the Year 8s are getting on with their sideshows. The head of year, Mr. Harvey, has wisely arranged two-hour stints for his enthusiastic workers, meaning that the creators of the shows could actually do two stints, provided that they either closed down or found a deputy between twelve and two. It seems to be working a treat. In the first room we see tombola, 'Guess the Weight of the Cake', mini skittles and table football – and they're loving it. More than one younger child is heard to announce, "I'm coming to Graysfield when I'm eleven," as they immerse themselves in the colourful activities. We move next door, and are spoilt for choice between magnetic darts, Junior Scrabble, treasure map and 'Guess the Doll's Name'.

We'll pop into one more room. Ah! Here we see the girls with their lucky dip. But they're ahead of the game. Having been advised to expect crowds, they have prepared not one lucky dip but two – one for nine-year-olds and over and another for younger visitors. The prizes have been specially selected as suitable for both girls and boys. And the girls have ensured plenty of helpers, so everything is working well.

Now let's take a look outside. As we approach the games field we can hear the shouts of boys – and some girls – on the six-a-side football pitch, while across the field we see two six-a-side netball games in full swing.

On an adjacent field we have lanes marked out for runners, and already, eager competitors are circuiting the field at varying speeds, while eagle-eyed prefects and sixth formers check their progress. We zoom in and spot two 'eager beavers' running in tandem at a moderate pace, red-faced and already bathed in sweat. As they pass the gate to the field, they seem to cast an anxious glance, before shaking their heads and continuing their run.

Everything seems to be progressing well. Looks like we're in for a really good day!

Jimmy could see Luke and Bren giving it a real go on the far side of the field. He waited till they came round and could now see that both of them, especially Luke, were struggling. Suddenly Brendan spotted Jimmy and let out a breathless cheer.

"Jimmy! What kept you, mate? We've done miles already!"

Jimmy started to explain, but then said, "Look guys, I'll tell you more as we run round. But first, where do I sign in?"

The boys pointed to a table near the field entrance, where two prefects were seated with various piles of paper in front of them.

"Show them your sponsor form," said Brendan, "then come back and join us. We've done seven laps already. But we'll carry on and do as many as we can, won't we, Luke?"

Luke nodded willingly, though he already looked shattered.

Jimmy placed his bag next to the boys' and trotted off to book in at the prefects' table.

"You're late, Jimmy," remarked Fred Briggs, a smiley-faced prefect, busy sorting papers.

Jimmy briefly explained that he had had to help an old lady who was ill on the bus. When he heard about the call for the paramedic, Fred's mood changed completely.

"Jimmy, you're a little star," beamed Fred. "With boys like you in the school we'll do well. Here, stick this on your shirt."

It was a sticker bearing Jimmy's name and confirming that he had signed in with his sponsor form – just part of the major organisation that Smithy had put in place to ensure that not only the running events, but indeed the whole day, ran like clockwork.

Jimmy thanked Fred, and ran off to join his mates on their run around the school field, but not before all three had gulped down a long and welcome swig of squash. Luke and Bren were amazed by Jimmy's story. But soon it was time to get back to some serious running.

The first lap was easy for Jimmy – and the second. But he was becoming increasingly aware that his two companions, especially Luke, were finding it harder and harder to keep going. The boys agreed to stop at their bags for a drink before completing what would be the final scheduled lap for Luke and Brendan. The drink energised everyone, and even Luke willingly agreed to carry on for a little while with Jimmy.

But eleven was the max for Luke, and twelve for Bren, meaning Jimmy still had five to do when his mates had finished. But he didn't mind. In fact, he suddenly realised that smiley prefect Fred had encouraged a sizeable group of spectators to cheer him on, telling them that he had already "done his bit on the way to school".

Jimmy was so inspired by the support he was receiving that he was actually surprised when Fred called to inform him that he had completed his ten laps. Jimmy stopped for a fresh swig and noticed that by now many Year 8s were joining in the run.

"Of course," thought Jimmy, "they started at eleven."

He went up to the table and checked that it would be OK for him to carry on alongside the Year 8s.

"Do as much as you like," quipped Fred, "but best to finish by twelve. Some of the Year 9s are really big and fast!"

Jimmy completed a further two laps before reckoning he needed to go and check out what Luke and Bren were doing – and of course see all the other activities that were taking place in Graysfield that day.

It was a crazy day – in the best possible sense. Everyone was determined to raise as much money as possible for the good causes they knew could benefit from all their efforts. The games field saw a constant stream of runners moving around the track at various speeds, each doing their bit to raise money. On an adjacent field, teams of footballers and netballers were sweating it out and thoroughly enjoying the competitions arranged for them by the enthusiastic games staff. Close by, one of the barbecues was serving dozens of hungry customers with sizzling burgers, hotdogs, fried onions and all the trimmings. Simply delicious!

Indoors, visitors enthused over the wonderful displays of artwork assembled in so short a time. And in the main hall, dozens of would-be Graysfield pupils were having enormous fun with steam engines, model cars and flying machines.

The dining hall had a steady stream of visitors, and food supplies, abundant at first, were by early afternoon becoming stretched. But everyone agreed the food delicious – and the waitress service, provided by Year 11 girls over the busy lunch period, was most welcome.

And – oh – the sideshows! Primary-aged siblings were simply spoilt for choice. The stalls were all reasonably priced, and 50p spent on a lucky dip was particularly good value, with very acceptable prizes of miniature novelty toys and games.

By early afternoon, the music staff, well-supplied with their own packed lunches, had already drawn up outline concerts for both younger and older pupils. It had been a win-win situation. Even the absolute beginners, like Lucy on the violin and Ben on the piano, had loved the experience and had delighted an enthusiastic and supportive audience.

Between one and two, Jimmy popped into the hall to support Matthew as he performed on his trumpet. And yes, it was 'Midnight in Moscow'. What a piece! Considering he had only been practising it for four weeks, it was a super effort. His teachers seemed thrilled by his performance.

Jimmy then moved away into the sports hall.

Suddenly he heard a familiar voice.

"Jimmy," cried Brendan excitedly, "your painting is up – and it's next to mine!"

Jimmy looked up to where Brendan was pointing. Sure enough, the 'Still Life' which he had painstakingly completed at home, copying his mum's bowl of fruit and using Brendan's paints, was displayed for all to see. Both boys whooped for joy.

Throughout the whole afternoon the boys thrilled to see the efforts everyone had put into this grand occasion. How great it was to see the many talents Graysfield had on show on that memorable day!

———————————

Throughout the day, Colin Smith had wandered around, supporting, encouraging, advising, applauding. Unflappable. He knew this was big. Many would be helped. He couldn't wait to see the final figures.

26

AN ASTONISHING RESULT

At last it was time to pack up. The head of games had arranged everything, and in fact most areas were cleared quite smoothly and quickly by those who had been operating there. The prefects carried their tables and chairs to the shed, all games equipment was collected and stored, and finally the last stragglers of energetic visiting youngsters revelling in their own green space on the school field had been kindly but firmly sent back to join their parents.

Colin thanked as many as he could for their great efforts. Some popped into the staff room for a 'cuppa' – and were delighted to notice a table full of cakes on plates. Colin had brought them up, seeing them left over at the end of the cake sale in the dining hall, and had provided them for his hungry colleagues. Any not picked up today would be popped into tins and kept for breaktime on Monday. Yes, he had thought of everything.

He downed his hot drink, picked up a cake himself and moved down to the school office. Even Colin had to knock there. The money counters had been locked into the office for security reasons and when the head of games entered, the secretary and her assistants had clearly been engrossed in sorting and counting hundreds of banknotes from the proceeds of the day. Loose coins had all been tipped into a large container. It would take too long to count, so Colin had made an arrangement with the local bank to use their counting machine to count the coins and deposit the money.

Most of the notes had been brought to the office during the day, to avoid a long haul for the counters at the end of the event. So when the head of games entered, the secretary gave him a warm, if tired, greeting.

"Just give us five minutes to tot up these totals, Colin," said Sue, "and you will see what we have raised in notes."

A short while later, she handed him a note. He glanced at the note and took a step back.

"You're joking!" he exclaimed.

"No, I was the final checker," replied Sue. "We've all three counted it. So that's right. And, of course, you've got loose change to come."

"I'll be back for that, and I'll have Rob with me."

Rob was the school bursar, rarely seen, but he would be on hand for this. Oh yes, he certainly would!

Rob had the cheques – at least those that had been handed over. A handful of sponsors had yet to fork out – but sufficient had been received to give a good indication of the kind of total raised.

Colin showed Rob the print-out from Sue. It showed the total amount in notes that had been taken on the day.

£ 20	£ 4,340
£ 10	£ 3,690
£ 5	£ 1,405

Total   £ 9,435

Rob had received twenty-seven cheques totalling £532.50. The total was already approaching ten thousand pounds, with loose cash and a few cheques still to come – by any standard, a major success.

The two men returned to the school office. Sue had transferred the loose coins to two strong containers. Rob and Colin took one each, thanked Sue and her staff and left for Rob's four-by-four parked ready outside.

"Must say, this machine's a beauty," remarked the head of games, when all the coins had been gobbled up and the total presented. "That would have taken hours to count."

"You're right; she *is* a beauty," replied Rob, "but so is today's result. I mean, just look at that total!"

"Fantastic!" agreed Colin. "Four thousand, seven hundred and eighty-four pounds and twenty-one pence. Add that to the near ten grand we had already. We can do a lot of good with that, for sure."

"Yes, and don't you forget what I said down at the 'Bird In Hand' t'other night," said Rob wryly.

For a moment Colin was taken aback. "You weren't serious, mate? I mean, you had had a few."

"Never been so serious in me life," replied Rob firmly. "I meant every penny."

Colin recalled what Rob had said: "Whatever you raise, I'll match it pound for pound." The head of games, not usually lost for words, was now.

"Ah, say no more," continued Rob. "I'll write you out a cheque tomorrow – after I've informed my bank manager; he likes to know what's going on."

Colin was about to say something when Rob carried on: "Just one condition. Like I said before, no names. That's how I want it. No, I mean it. I'm Mr. Anonymous. Please. Thanks, Colin!"

"OK, Rob. All I can say is, it's very gen—"

"Mate, I'm only giving back what's been given to me. I've been blessed in my life, that's for sure."

Colin knew where his friend was coming from. Rob had inherited a large country house with seven acres of land in early adulthood, and had over time transformed much of the land to produce saleable fruit and vegetables on a large scale. The business had taken off following a call from a neighbouring landowner which had resulted in a pooling of resources and manpower, as well as access to multiple trade outlets built up over many years by the new business partner.

In short, Rob was not short of a quid or two. But Colin was one of few people who knew the extent of Rob's wealth. Put simply, the football coach was a trusted friend, and this was why, knowing his passion for Graysfield School, Rob had offered to match the final total pound for pound.

Since taking on the post of bursar at Graysfield, Rob had eased off on his business activities, content in the knowledge that there had long been established a highly competent and productive workforce to keep up the momentum in the joint venture. But he did enjoy supporting worthy causes; it seemed to add so much purpose – and sheer fun – to his life.

And what could be more worthy a cause than Graysfield?

By close of school on Monday, all outstanding cheques and contributions had been handed in and totalled up.

Cash	£ 14,261,46
Cheques	£ 570.50
Total	**£ 14,831.96**

Colin showed the total to Rob in Tuesday morning coffee break.

"Sorry, mate," said Rob. "No can do."

Colin's jaw dropped – but only a little. He knew Rob. He glanced, slightly anxiously, to his mate, and, yes, was relieved to see the very slightest twinkle in his eye.

"Can't be dealing with those odd pence," continued Rob. "Let's round it up." There was still a bit of tease in Rob's voice. "Nah, let's be doin' with it. I said that before I saw the effort you all put in the other day. Superb, I say. That's fifteen grand."

And before Colin could respond, Rob pronounced in clearest tones, "Double fifteen... that's thirty thousand this fine school has raised in one day. Well done, Colin!"

The head of games was almost speechless, but just said, "Thanks, mate," and poured himself another coffee.

27

LEADING QUESTIONS

A full staff meeting had been fixed for Tuesday. Main business: allocation of monies raised on Saturday. Ideas would be invited and serious recommendations discussed. Final choices would be made on Thursday at a meeting of all key players.

Thursday's meeting was lively, but largely with everyone singing from the same hymn sheet. Basically, the school was largely new build, so structurally sound and generally enjoying most key facilities. But there were three main areas where funding could go a long, long way: IT and computers; the library; and sport, including money for kits.

It was proposed that the thirty thousand pounds should be split three ways, with the heads of I.T., the library service and games being given responsibility for expenses of up to ten thousand pounds in their own speciality.

All staff involved were budgetary experts, and everyone knew they could be relied upon to purchase equipment which was high quality but also at the best price. Colin Smith and the head of girls' games, Helen Hill, immediately agreed to split their share equally, so that both boys' and girls' games would benefit from an injection of five thousand pounds towards kit and equipment.

Colin was clear about his share. New kits had been the main motivation for having a special school event. The school already possessed one set for each year group. Now, with a hundred and eighty children pushing for places in each year, a second set for all ages would be a tremendous boost, enabling double the number to look forward to playing in a school team. The coach had already costed strips at four to five hundred pounds per set. With five Key Stage 3 and 4 years as well as the sixth form, that would be three thousand pounds on kits. The extra teams would need more practices, meaning probably more footballs and other equipment. It was not difficult to see how the boys' five thousand pounds could be spent.

Of course, new kit and a second team would require fixtures. Colin had long decided that the magnificent effort which had been invested in 'Graysfield's Got Talent' deserved a special reward. And who better to confer with over a possible sporting treat than his counterparts at that friendly, sports-loving school, St. Mary's?

St. Mary's were only too eager to help. They had fields, facilities and staff – and, of course, a rather unique Parent-Teacher Association team for refreshments. They just needed to agree a date.

St. Mary's suggested three possibilities for the spring term, and would consult local schools regarding tournaments in both football and netball and choice of dates. Colin consulted Helen, after which both emailed through their available dates and waited for St. Mary's to reply.

Three weeks later, the football coach heard back from St. Mary's. Tournaments would be held two weeks apart, in the spring term, and would, as this was a starter, involve Year 7s only, though Graysfield were welcome to send two teams for both netball and football. Colin was more than happy with this. Enthusiasm was at fever pitch in Year 7, and although Helen and he had more than enough in Years 8 and 9 for single teams, those year groups already had a full fixture list including tournaments and were well used to rotating squads over the season. The football coach wasted no time in informing the boys, and football practices in the coming weeks became keener and more thrilling than ever.

There was one decision Colin was particularly keen to get right. The 'A' team had a natural captain in Charlie Matthews. Not only a gifted footballer, Charlie had an excellent temperament, was never fazed and knew the game inside-out. A good captain.

The coach knew choice of captain was important. A good captain could not only bring the best out of the players, his attitude could be reflected also in the way the team acquitted themselves on the pitch. But most of the contenders for the 'B' team had not yet played for the school at all. That could be a disadvantage for a prospective captain.

Then Colin thought of Jimmy. Yes, he had responded rashly to Kai in the training session, but he seemed to have put that behind him now and learnt from his mistake. He did seem to be turning into a decent lad. And Colin had been particularly impressed when Fred had told him about Jimmy's heroics with the old lady on the bus, and how he had then come straight to the games field to complete not ten but twelve laps for 'Graysfield's Got Talent'. *Yes,* thought Smithy. *Impressive.*

It could be argued that Jimmy was probably good enough for the first team. But his determined attitude could well be put to best use if he were to captain the seconds. Though he might be surprised, the football coach believed Jimmy would look on it as an honour to lead the team.

28

THE ST. MARY'S TOURNAMENT

Jimmy was thrilled to be a part of the football tournament and excited at having been chosen to captain one of the teams. The tournament was to be a competition between eight teams, including two each from Graysfield and St. Mary's. Smithy had booked a coach to take the two teams to the event, and as it approached St. Mary's, Martin thought of one or two words of encouragement to share with his team before kick-off.

On arrival, Martin was handed a programme for the day. The competition would take place on two adjacent pitches, with the two 'A' teams joining Perry Mead and Oakwell on one pitch, while the 'B' teams, Banfield and Sheldon, would contest on the other. Graysfield 'A' were first up against Oakwell, while on the other pitch St. Mary's 'B' were to play Banfield. This would allow Martin and his team to watch their future opponents before taking on Sheldon in their first match.

He kept his words brief. "Watch the players you're likely to be against," he said. "Look for any weaknesses and try to play on to them when you get on. Keep warm while you are off the pitch – and then, let's give it some!"

At last it was time for Jimmy's 'B' team to start their tournament against Sheldon. Graysfield 'A' had come through a close tussle to beat Oakwell 2-1, with a superb winning goal by Abdoulkader, and so it would be encouraging to keep up the good start.

But Sheldon looked like no pushovers. They had two tall defenders and a burly-looking striker, and the boys guessed they would have a game on their hands.

How right they were! Within a minute, Graysfield were a goal behind, when the burly striker received a good through pass and muscled his way through the Graysfield defence, scoring easily from ten yards.

Jimmy knew this would be a tough game, and tried hard to rally his troops. But this was an early hammer-blow – and Sheldon really had their tails up. The Graysfield defence were doing their best, Martin giving great support from the touchline, and Jimmy and Ravi particularly prominent. But just before half-time, the pressure told and Sheldon scored a fine second goal.

The interval was short, but just long enough for Martin to individually encourage each member of his team to keep going – "…and then," he said, "you never know!"

The second half began with Jimmy's 'B' team really putting up a fight against their strong, talented opponents. A quick raid from the right found Kevin, who shot straight and hopefully. It was too quick for the keeper, and Kevin's rising shot found the back of the net. Now the score was 1-2, and they were back in the game. The response, however, was swift and sharp. Sheldon upped their game, and launched attacks down both flanks. The Graysfield defence, with Jimmy outstanding, were under intense pressure, and only three fine saves from Billy in goal and a skilful goal-line clearance from Jimmy prevented it from becoming a rout.

Graysfield were holding on – but they were still behind. With three minutes to go, Jimmy moved upfield in support of what looked like a promising attack, hoping to help force an equalizer. He received the ball on the edge of the penalty area and struck it firmly towards goal. But the keeper had it covered. He caught the ball and quickly launched a counterattack.

Jimmy raced back, but was caught out of position, the Sheldon forwards driving on menacingly. A right-wing cross found the burly striker, and he deftly shifted the ball to his stronger left foot, ready to shoot. The keeper made a gallant effort, but the striker was only eight yards out, and power and placement were too much. The ball crashed into the back of the net for 3-1.

There wasn't even time to restart. It was a defeat for Jimmy's team in their first match. Martin ushered the boys off the field towards their bags and bottles. "Take in plenty of liquid while I talk to you," said the coach. "We have only a short break before we play Banfield. But listen up. We have already watched our next two opponents, so we have the advantage of having studied their strengths and weaknesses. Any observations?"

"I would say Sheldon look better than either Banfield or St. Mary's 'B'," said Kevin. "Sheldon were really tough opponents."

Many heads nodded.

"I think you are right," agreed Martin, "which is why it was good to watch Banfield and St. Mary's play. Now, even though we have lost our first match, we can still qualify for the semifinals if we beat both of those teams."

Some of the boys cheered up noticeably.

"As I said, we are about to play Banfield, who lost heavily to St. Mary's. You might be a bit leggy, but if we can start strongly and take our chances, then hopefully you will have enough quality to fend them off in the second half. After that we have a break before our final group match. Ah, the referee is calling you over. All the best, boys!"

Jimmy led the way back on to the pitch. He won the toss and decided to kick towards the end where they had scored their goal against Sheldon. It seemed to pay off. Within five minutes Graysfield had scored twice against a none-too-confident Banfield defence.

Martin studied the body language of his players. They were playing in second gear, yet they were two up. The opposition had little to offer, and rarely ventured out of their own half. The match was quiet for a while, with little action at either end. But then a minute before half-time, Danny sent a peach of a ball through to Henry. The striker collected the ball in his stride and skilfully drew the keeper before coolly slotting it into the unguarded net. Shortly after, the referee blew for half-time.

Martin decided, with his team cruising at 3-0, that it would be a good time to send on the two subs who had been waiting all morning to get on.

"Bill, Tommy," he called, "I'd like you to take off your tops and go and have the game of your lives!"

Bill Bradbury and Tommy Newton were ready in a flash. You'd think it was Wembley and the Cup Final!

"Ready for action, sir!" called Tommy comically – and you could see this would go down as one of the highlights of his young life.

"Just go and do your stuff then," said Martin. "The rest of you – well done, keep it up and don't let it slip in the second half!"

It was not the most exciting second half, but Graysfield did enough to win comfortably, snuffing out the Banfield attack and adding a fourth goal through Kevin, from a fine through ball from Brendan, near the end.

Bill and Tommy came off red-cheeked and heavy-legged – but that experience had meant the world to them. And the honour of playing for their school team was something they would never forget.

Time for a rest! Martin had brought some half-oranges for the boys, which he now handed round, before advising them to fetch their tracksuit tops and take a restful break before the St. Mary's match. Just before they were due back on to the pitch, the 'B'-team coach called his troops together.

"I trust you feel a little refreshed, boys," he said. "You know, this is a rare opportunity: a time when you can play against different levels of opposition in one day. Think of it as a footballing learning curve. You've played two matches – you saw different abilities, and so were probably able to work out for yourselves different tactics, different ways to play. That should help you against St. Mary's. Plus the fact that you have already watched them play. So enjoy the game, show what you can do and what you've learnt. Okay, off you go, enjoy!"

The boys ran on to take on St. Mary's, knowing that a win should see them through to the semis.

29

A Crazy Game

The early stages of the match were uneventful, as both teams tried to size up their opponents, in their search for a place in the semi-finals. But no one could have predicted what was to happen next. From a well-taken corner by Callum, Henry connected brilliantly first time on the volley to place the ball past the helpless St. Mary's keeper and into the back of the net. Spurred on by this success, Graysfield scored a second through Danny, following a good searching through ball from Luke.

Within a minute Graysfield were three goals to the good. Jimmy crossed accurately from the right, and Scott, ready near the far post, calmly steered the ball into the net.

Graysfield were now coasting, and may have relaxed a little. Whatever it was, St. Mary's centre-half fed their left-winger, and the winger, quick as lightning, outpaced the Graysfield defender to run on and send a scorching shot past Billy in goal.

Worse was still to come. Almost from the kick-off, Henry was dispossessed, and the St. Mary's right-winger strode forward to send an unstoppable shot into the corner of the net for 3-2. Keen to retake the initiative, Graysfield stormed forward, and Henry shot firmly towards the far corner. The St. Mary's keeper was up for it, however, pouncing on the ball and quickly releasing a strong forward kick down the right. The St. Mary's winger was on to it in a flash, and caught out the Graysfield defence as they hurried back to defend their goal. It was too late. Before they could re-form, the winger sent a scorching shot past Billy for an equaliser which five minutes ago had seemed most unlikely. Almost immediately after that, the referee blew for half-time.

Martin knew his half-time talk must be short and to the point. "Take a good drink and listen up," he said. "You showed your quality in the early stages, but you let them back in through making errors. Now we're starting again. Pretend it's 0-0. In a sense it is. So you're now going to start afresh with your best game. That means in defence as well as attack, throughout the match. Right lads – off you go. Enjoy!"

Off went the lads, and the second half got underway. It was a much tighter affair now, with neither team giving much away. A good attempt came in from the St. Mary's striker, which Billy tipped over the bar. Jimmy made sure his teammates were tightly marking their opponents, as a St. Mary's winger prepared to take the corner. It was floated up well, but slightly too near the keeper, who advanced and caught it cleanly. Remembering his coach's words, Billy told his backs to keep it tight, and then sent a high, accurate kick towards the right flank.

Callum carefully watched the flight of the ball and, as it dropped, moved quickly to make first connection. He had already had the beating of his opposite number twice before in the game without making it count. This time he was determined to do better. He deftly flicked the ball past his opponent, running on to collect it and dribble on down the wing. He was banking on Kevin or Henry moving up in support. He glanced up. Henry was close by but marked, whereas Kevin was just the far side of the penalty spot and available. Callum crossed strongly, and Kevin, eye on the ball, made a clean contact before releasing a firm drive towards the bottom corner. The St. Mary's keeper made a brave attempt to save, but Kevin's shot was clean and accurate, and sped into the net to give Graysfield the lead.

With just six minutes remaining, Jimmy encouraged his teammates to keep things tight, and with Martin cheering them on from the touchline, Graysfield were determined to hold on to their lead. Indeed, apart from a snap shot from the St. Mary's number nine, which soared over the bar, the Graysfield defence remained largely untroubled, and the team held on to secure a memorable 4-3 victory and a place against the St. Mary's 'A' team in the semifinal.

––––––––––––––––

The tournament organisers had planned it so that there would be a good break between the group matches and the final stages. Tired bodies and aching limbs needed rest and refreshment, so as well as inviting visitors to bring packed lunches, there were a number of tables and kiosks available where hot and cold drinks and light snacks could be purchased.

Martin knew from experience that a boy whose stomach is satisfied will listen far better than one who is desperate for food. So first things first. Most boys had brought their own packed food and drinks, so attending to that and other necessaries was priority.

He also allowed time for them to wander round and chat to mates in the 'A' team, or simply to view St. Mary's pleasant fields, which, unlike their own, had attractive wooded areas interspersed with meadow land, as well as plenty of space for casual games and other outdoor activities.

Fifteen minutes before restart, Martin got Jimmy and the vice captain, Danny, to round up the troops before delivering his eve of battle message.

30

A Big Decision

Once all the boys were assembled and ready, Martin's words were cheery and to the point. "You've done better than I expected, to be honest," the coach said. "Well done, lads. Now anything else is a bonus! Mr. Smith has watched both St. Mary's teams, and tells me they play similar styles of football. You will have noticed, when their 'B' team broke, they used the wings quite a lot. So do the 'A's. Watch for that. Try to close down their wide men to prevent them crossing the ball. As some of you will remember from playing them before, they do have one particularly athletic defender. Try to get the play away from him if possible. Otherwise they are not so speedy at the back. They certainly don't like the winger getting in behind to knock the balls back for the forwards. Those of you who've played them before" – and here he looked at Jimmy and Ravi – "try to remember what you learnt about your opponents then – their strengths and weaknesses. Think clearly; get your head clear to make the right decisions.

"One final word, boys," concluded the 'B'-team coach. "Remember the F.A. Cup. Everyone likes an underdog. And sometimes, as you may well know, the underdog wins through! Anyway, I see the ref is on the pitch already. So off you go – and enjoy!"

The boys, spurred on by their coach's words, ran on to the pitch. Yes, they were underdogs all right – Graysfield 'B' team playing against St. Mary's 'A'. But, as coach had said, underdogs do sometimes win through. Well, they would give it their best shot – and just see what might happen.

The match began cautiously. St. Mary's were playing the ball around with confidence, while at the same time looking for any weaknesses in their opponents' defence. But Jimmy, playing in his now customary position of right-back, was marshalling the defenders well. A keen eye for detail, he ensured as far as possible that key opponents were tightly marked. He brought enough players back for set pieces to allow himself to watch out for the unexpected – a sudden forward run from an opponent or a shot to be cleared off the line.

So as the first half wore on, the St. Mary's team, though enjoying most of the possession, were becoming slightly frustrated in their efforts to break down a stubborn Graysfield defence. Then, three minutes before half-time, a corner from the right found St. Mary's short, stocky striker. He quickly controlled the ball before unleashing a powerful drive which was heading towards the top right corner. Fortunately, Billy, in goal, already warned by Jimmy of the player's threat, watched the ball all the way before leaping to strong-hand it away for another corner. This one was comfortably cleared, and a minute or so later the referee brought the half to an end, with Graysfield still very much holding their own.

The second half was similarly tight, but as the game wore on, some of the St. Mary's players began to tire, and the extra fitness regimes encouraged by the Graysfield coaches appeared to be paying off. Gradually Graysfield saw more of the ball, and it was now conceivable that they might even snatch a winner. Jimmy, still cautious to keep things tight at the back, received a ball from Billy before feeding Callum on the right. Callum easily beat his tiring opposite number before continuing on down the wing. As he approached the St. Mary's penalty area, he noticed their defender hesitant and holding back. Remembering his coach's words, he suddenly sprinted past the full-back, reached the goal line and turned. He then hooked the ball back, causing confusion to the St. Mary's defenders. Kevin, ready and alert, ran forward to meet the ball and, with a smart dink, rounded the keeper and ran the ball into the net.

The touchline supporters were ecstatic, and even Martin could be seen pumping his fists in excitement. 1-0 with just four minutes to go. Jimmy called, shouted, warned and encouraged his team-mates, as they now fought for every ball to secure victory. Finally the ref blew the whistle for a narrow but well-deserved win.

The players were over the moon as they returned to Martin and attacked their drink bottles before lying back on the turf to recover their energy.

"Boys," said Martin, as his young fighters lay exhausted around him, "that was magnificent. Take a short rest, then you're in the final – against your school mates!"

Yes, Smithy's 'A' team had just narrowly beaten Sheldon 2-1, to set up an intriguing all-Graysfield final to round off this enthralling tournament. Martin knew his team would need absolutely no motivation from him for this one. They would be fully pumped up by the dream of a famous victory over their higher-ranked schoolmates.

It couldn't get much better than that!

Martin this time left it until the last possible minute before rousing his team to play their friends in the final. They had left the field shattered, so every moment of their short break had been precious. But now the referee was on the pitch, and the coach rallied his boys: "Go and give everyone a Graysfield showpiece." Final swigs of juice and they were off to show what they could do.

It was a rather curious start to the match. The players on both sides knew each other's game well, and although the 'A' team were generally more skilful players, the 'B's had improved so much that now there was not that much to differentiate between the two teams. Certainly the 'B's' defence, who had been improving in every game, were surprising their opponents by their tight marking and decisive clearances. And when Kai did manage to escape his markers to send in a firm drive, Billy in goal watched it all the way and made a confident save.

So the match remained goalless at half-time.

As the second half wore on, it became clear that a single goal would probably decide the match. And then there was a key moment…

The 'A' strikers, Kai and Abdul, had been well shackled by the busy and increasingly competent 'B' defence. But in a rare moment, Charlie, working his way down the right, spotted Kai for once available and unmarked. He sent a strong, accurate pass in his direction.

Kai, by now on the edge of the box, moved in on the ball and, looking up, spotted his chance. Taking careful aim, he made a good connection. His firm drive rose then dipped on its way to goal. The keeper, slightly off his line, was beaten. Jimmy, quick and cool, was back on the goal line, covering. But the pace on the ball could well beat him. He keenly watched as it dipped towards the goal and, reaching the ball, got as much as he could on it in an effort to keep it out. Margins were fine. But as he made contact, Jimmy knew that the ball had crossed the line. His clearance was to no avail. It was a goal.

The referee, close to the corner of the penalty box, hesitated, unsure as to whether the ball had crossed the line or not. He looked hopefully towards his linesman, but got no joy there. The linesman, too, was uncertain – and, worse, was dithering. But his flag remained down, if not firmly so, and the referee allowed play to continue, signalling a throw-in from where Jimmy's relieving kick had crossed the touchline.

Jimmy was in a quandary. He was clear in his mind: the ball had crossed the line and a goal should be awarded. But if he went and told the referee, wasn't he letting his team down after all their effort? He could play on, but he was not happy. He knew the truth of the matter. No, he could *not* carry on. He *must* tell it as it had really happened.

The ball had yet to be thrown in – Jimmy's clearance had been powerful enough to clear the spectators on the touchline. He hurried over to the referee, with the linesman close by.

"The ball went over the line; it was a goal," he said.

The referee, surprised at Jimmy's honesty, hesitated for a moment, before thanking Jimmy, raising his hand and pointing to the centre spot to signify a goal.

The 'A's were, to say the least, relieved. The 'B's were deflated. Jimmy tried hard to encourage his team to keep going – and they did – but now the ball was twice as heavy and the sky much less blue. It was a crushing blow for a team that had fought all the way for every ball. No one knew this keener than Jimmy. As the full impact of what he had done hit him, he began to doubt the wisdom of his decision. He looked around at his teammates. Everyone was still giving their all but now clearly struggling. He felt himself welling up inside.

Then the referee blew to end the match.

As Jimmy returned with his teammates to Martin, his head was just a blur. Distantly, he heard cries of delight from the 'A' team. Close to hand were his teammates, some putting on a brave face, others with tears in their eyes. Everyone had aches and pains, knocks and scratches.

This is where a coach shows his worth, thought Martin, as he tried to console his battered band of fighters. "Guys, sit down, lie down, I don't care, but listen up. I asked for a Graysfield showpiece. You gave us that. You were immense today. You lads can hold your heads high – *very* high. What a game you gave us!"

Then turning to Jimmy, but still addressing all of the boys, he said, "Jimmy, that was one of the most courageous decisions I have witnessed by any player, let alone an eleven-year-old. You certainly can hold your head high. You showed character and guts – *and*, boys," he said, facing them all compassionately, "your captain made the right decision. I don't think Jimmy could have lived with himself had he known he had denied his schoolmates a goal they had rightly scored. No, it was the right decision. And it's my reckoning that those boys in the 'A' team will respect him for it."

"Boys, you've been great today," he concluded. "Now, gather your things, and I want you all to follow me to the awards ceremony."

31

MAN WITH A MESSAGE

Martin led Jimmy and the team to the specially prepared 'presentation area' alongside the main field. As most schools had already completed their games, a large number of players, coaches and spectators had already gathered – some adult supporters on fold-up chairs or picnic blankets, others on the grass which, on account of the recent fine weather, was warm and dry.

Centrally, and set back within the presentation area, two dining tables had been placed end to end to make a presentation table holding trophies and other awards. Considering there had only been six schools and eight teams involved, Jimmy was probably not alone in thinking that there were rather a lot of trophies there for the occasion.

Martin noticed Smithy with his boys, and ushered his team towards them. Altogether, a good crowd of families and friends had come along in support. They were delighted at what they had seen, and were now keen and excited to watch the awards.

They did not have long to wait.

The St. Mary's headmaster rose from his chair and stepped towards the microphone.

"A very warm welcome to you all," he began. "Thank you all so much for being a part of our very first St. Mary's schools football tournament. We have had a wonderful day, with some great action on the field as well as superb support from the touchline. I would particularly like to thank the officials who have given up their time to take charge of the matches and so have enabled the day to run so smoothly.

"Hopefully this could be the first of many such occasions. But first, I am delighted to welcome someone who is highly regarded throughout the local footballing world. In his early years he captained top team Solway Rangers, before being spotted by the scouts of several league clubs. Sadly, a motorcycle injury cut short his playing career, although he has successfully continued to manage Solway over many seasons, taking them to three local league championships as well as enabling them to win several area trophies during that time.

"So, this gentleman is a winner – and a leader. But he is more than that. In fact, much more. When his career was cut short, of course he was devastated. As were his family and friends. As were *we all*. But very soon this remarkable man developed strategies to come to terms with his new situation. He went back to the drawing-board, as we say, and he rethought his life and his prospects. Just one of the brilliant ideas he has developed has been to set up centres where children with disabilities might enjoy playing some of the sports and games they love, just as all of you have done today. Now this gentleman has generously agreed to give up some of his precious time to join us here. And I for one am so looking forward to hearing what he has to say to us. Ladies and gentlemen, girls and boys, a very warm welcome, please, to... *Richard Adley*."

A warm applause followed. After such an introduction, even those with the shortest of attention spans were eager to hear what this 'local legend' had to say.

Richard Adley steered his wheelchair towards the microphone.

"My friends," he began, "it is a great joy to be with you all here today. I have seen the efforts, the skill, the keen determination of you all. You are a credit to your schools, and they must be fine coaches who have produced such splendid representatives of their schools as you are. But what I have most enjoyed is the spirit in which you have played today." Then, turning to the referees and linemen seated alongside him, he added, with a twinkle in his eye, "And not too many red cards, I trust, gentlemen?"

The referees shook their heads.

"Good discipline," said one.

"Hard fought, but in a good spirit," said another.

Richard Adley turned again to face the teams. "The headmaster is right," he continued, "when he says I needed to rethink my life – or maybe *rediscover* it. You could even say that life itself has suggested ways in which I might do this. I certainly realised I had to rethink my dreams and aspirations. Yes, I had dreams – *big* dreams. But do you know what? It is good to strive to do your best in whatever you do (and you all have surely done that today). But not everyone can be a winner. There must be some who do not quite achieve that. So then, does that make them any worse as people? Of course not. In fact there is, I have learnt, such a thing as a good loser. Or a good sport. And that, I guess, is someone who is gracious in defeat and who remains true to their inner beliefs and values. Not always easy – especially when there are trophies at stake!

"But now, enough talking from me – I have the delightful task of presenting some awards today. And as you have all performed so valiantly, I see that the generous St. Mary's organising team have provided an engraved commemorative medallion for each and every one who has taken part in today's tournament. That's players, coaches and officials."

One by one, the referees and other officials were acknowledged and duly applauded. And then, in turn, the names of each of the participating teams were called out, and the boys and their coaches filed out to the podium, each to receive their medallion. This was placed around their neck in honour of their participation in the event. It took several minutes, but it was worth it. Everyone's efforts had been acknowledged. Everyone had something to take away from the event which would say, "I was there. That was a special day for me."

"And now," beamed Mr. Adley, "the winners. We have already said, there can only be one winning team. You are all valued and have made your mark. But the winning team are... *Graysfield 'A'*. Very well done!"

Riotous applause ensued, as the Graysfield 'A' team followed their coach to the presentation area. Smithy then modestly stood aside to follow the team up to the podium. Each team member this time received a small silver trophy inscribed with details of the tournament, before the captain was handed a large silver cup draped with red, white and blue ribbons, the reward for the team's achievement. Charlie thanked Mr. Adley before turning to the crowd and thrusting his trophy-laden hands high into the air. The response was deafening.

"Well done, Graysfield!"

"Champions!"

"Well deserved!"

How pleased, how proud they all felt.

Mr. Adley continued applauding for a while. But then he gently raised his hand.

"Friends," he said, "there is one more thing I wish to say. I mentioned earlier the importance of being a good loser – and, generally, sportsmanship. Yes, that is so important. Well, you know, I am a very lucky man. Yes, I am! Because, knowing I was coming here today (and what a joy and an honour it has been, thank you all)" – he turned to St. Mary's headmaster, smiled broadly and raised his hand in gratitude – "I decided I wanted to bring along something myself, just in case I were to spot some act of sportsmanship which I reckoned to be just a little above and beyond. Something special. Something generous, noble and honourable. And – do you know, friends? – yes, I am a lucky man. Because I have seen something today which I can definitely rank in that category. Something which required guts and courage. True guts, true courage. It was something which, once done, actually cost that team not just the match but the trophy.

"I am referring, of course," continued Mr. Adley, "to the final match: Graysfield 'A' team versus Graysfield 'B'. A cracking match! The stuff of which heroes are made. And yes, I've known some in my time. Nothing to choose between the teams, no quarter given. And then – as often happen in these close affairs – a touch of class. A tremendous shot, good enough to win any match. And what happens? Well, you wouldn't believe it, but yes, perhaps the shortest player on the pitch somehow – don't ask me how – he gets over there and clears the ball – yes, really whacks it, sends it to kingdom come, way off the pitch and over the heads of the spectators. Everyone, officials included, thinks it's a terrific goal-line clearance. Did I say everyone? Well, no, not quite everyone. There's one who knows otherwise. Probably the only person in the ground who really knows whether that ball had crossed the goal-line or not. Yes, the one who made the clearance.

"He knew the ball had crossed the line. Okay, marginally, but *he knew*. He also knew he could carry on playing and no one might ever have known the truth. So, what did he do? Well, I guess there was a bit of wrestling within. *Am I not throwing the game away? Surely, I'm*

*"Well done, Jimmy," said the V.I.P. visitor,
as Jimmy received his trophy.*

letting down my team who have played so manfully? But no, he knew he must do the right thing – tell it as it happened. And that is what he did – risking the flak and feeling from his team-mates – and of course the trophy itself. *But he did.*

"To me, what he did – and I've been through a bit – was as important as any match-winning feat. Because he showed courage and character in his actions. That, to me, was true sportsmanship of the highest class. Yes, I'm a lucky man, because now I can go back home without this big, heavy bag I've been carrying round all day – because I'm about to offload it on to some of you.

"I would like to invite all the Graysfield 'B' team up to the rostrum, each to receive a trophy for sportsmanship, because, as far as I can tell, they may well have had thoughts about the decision their player made, but they showed true sportsmanship in accepting that decision and its consequences. Boys, please step forward to receive your awards."

Jimmy proudly led his team back to the rostrum. Richard Adley shifted slightly in his wheelchair and removed a dark covering to reveal a large open sports bag containing a set of protectively wrapped awards, one for each player. Amid gasps from the audience, the boys each in turn moved forward to receive them. As each came forward, Mr. Adley removed the wrapper to reveal a small silver trophy inscribed with the words "FOR SPORTSMANSHIP" on the base, with room for further inscriptions such as name of the player or school.

"Well done, Jimmy," said the V.I.P. visitor, as Jimmy received his trophy – and hearing these words from such a man as this felt so good.

As Jimmy returned, proudly clutching his trophy, to the Graysfield group, the entire crowd seemed to be applauding.

32

A COACH LOST FOR WORDS

Just approaching the Graysfield crowd, yet still a short distance behind them, was… the old lady, Mary Treasure. She was wheeling a shopping trolley.

Jimmy bypassed the Graysfield group and moved quickly to greet her. But before he could reach her, she exclaimed, "Jimmy! I'm so glad I've made it. And you've won a trophy!"

Jimmy looked modestly at the trophy he was clutching in his left hand while his right hand was helping the old lady steer her trolley towards the Graysfield crowd.

"Oh… yes," he agreed, as they reached the edge of the Graysfield crowd.

Jimmy reckoned it might be a little tricky returning to his original spot near Martin and his team-mates, so he found the old lady a spare folding chair which had been provided for the crowd, and sat down next to her and her trolley to hear the closing moments of the event. Looking across the crowd, he could see that Martin was surrounded by his excited team showing him their trophies.

Mr. Adley, having finished speaking, had made way for the headmaster to give his closing remarks. The 'B' team were by now settling back in their places, and Martin, Jimmy noticed, was looking a little perplexed. Maybe he should leave the old lady for a moment to join him and the team for the final minutes. As he hesitated, he noticed Martin looking round. The coach caught sight of Jimmy and raised his hand as if to say, "OK, I see where you are," before turning back to his team.

But moments later Martin looked back towards Jimmy again. This time he looked even more bewildered than before. He seemed to be looking closely, as if he were checking something.

As Jimmy watched, the coach got up and slowly walked towards him. But Martin was not looking at Jimmy. He appeared incredulous. Jimmy was puzzled.

The coach drew nearer. He looked carefully, *very* carefully, at the old lady, who was sorting items in her shopping trolley. Now he stood in front of her, as she still rummaged in her bag. For a moment he just stood staring at her, as she went on to examine the contents of the trolley.

Jimmy had never heard his coach squeak before. If anything, Martin had a deeper voice than Smithy – in fact, deeper than the headmaster. But now he squeaked. It was actually a cross between a squeak and a gasp. A sort of gasp-squeak.

"Gr— an?"

The old lady, rummaging, had heard something. Something vaguely familiar. She looked up. And then... a moment of pure magic.

"M— Martin!" – almost a whisper, sheer amazement. Then, "MARTIN!" – a much stronger response, one of true joy.

"Gran! After so long. Oh, Gran...!" was all the totally mesmerised coach could say.

"Martin! My dear, dear boy!" was the equally mystified response.

Jimmy could only watch on in amazement, as his coach hugged and hugged the old lady. Did he imagine it, or was there a tear in the coach's eyes? This was clearly a moment to savour. It was now becoming increasingly clear to Jimmy that this old lady, whom he had casually met on a bus some time ago, was none other than the gran of his team coach. Clearly the coach was greatly moved and delighted to have found his wonderful long-lost gran in such an astonishing way. It was a priceless moment, one that Jimmy would never forget.

For Martin and Mary, it was not just that they were meeting up for the first time in almost two years. Martin had a lifetime's experiences to share with his gran. His life had been turned around, transformed – and he wanted to share all that with the one who had meant so much to him for so long. That would surely take time. But he was determined to start right away.

33

KIND WORDS AND TASTY SAUSAGES

"And now, I do hope as many of you as possible will join us for a buffet in the dining hall." These were the only meaningful words Jimmy heard the headmaster utter, as he reeled from witnessing the 'old lady on the bus' reunited with her long-lost grandson, who just happened to be his football coach.

Martin, still shocked, at least recovered sufficiently to say, "Jimmy, I would like you to lead your team to the dining hall. I shall escort my gran, and we will meet up with you all shortly."

Jimmy duly returned to his mates, and escorted them to the hall. And what a feast it was! Everything you could want, be you adult or child, was laid out in buffet form in the centre of the hall, while to the side, kitchen staff were cheerfully handing pre-poured cold drinks to the teams, and adults queued for tea and coffee on the other side of the hall.

But that was not all. At the far end of the hall, away from the 'crowd', three very large kitchen containers, each manned by a uniformed kitchen worker, held sausages, chips and beans which the staff were merrily shovelling on to the plates of those young players who preferred it hot! Which most, especially Graysfield, certainly did. A feast indeed!

Most of Jimmy's team 'went hot', and then found a couple of side tables to share. Jimmy was just tucking into his sausages when he noticed Martin escorting the old lady into the hall. The coach placed the shopping trolley next to the old lady's coat, which he hung up at the end of the hall. Then the two of them approached the buffet table, where they filled their plates with welcome treats.

As the teams sat enjoying their sausages, Jimmy overheard a conversation nearby.

"I wouldn't have done that," said Henry. "It cost us the match – and the tournament."

"That's right," said Kevin. "And after we'd put in all that effort."

Then Jimmy heard a third voice, quieter and more deliberate. It was Ravi.

"I appreciate all that," he said, "but clearly Jimmy knew the ball had crossed the line. One thing I know about Jimmy is, he's always honest. I like him for that. I respect that in him. He had to be true to himself. Yes, he had to do what he did."

When Ravi was serious, people listened.

Aw, thanks, Ravi, thought Jimmy.

He then heard no more – apart from the scraping of knives on plates and the cheerful banter of boys whose craving for 'food, glorious food' was actually being satisfied.

Then, towards the end of the meal, Jimmy looked up and saw Kai coming towards him.

"Jimmy, how cool was that!" said Kai. "Thanks for telling the ref about the goal. All the team were amazed. Jus' wanna thank you for that."

Jimmy, having heard Ravi's comments, had recovered his confidence. "Kai, it *was* a goal – yes, an excellent goal. You struck it so well; it was a match-winner all the way. Well done!"

The two boys, already on good terms following their chats with Mr. Smith, were now even closer friends. It was a friendship built on the respect each had for the other.

Jimmy was just polishing off his sausages, beans and chips when he felt a tap on the shoulder. It was Smithy.

"Jimmy," said the football coach, "I can't tell you how proud we all are of you. I had an idea the ball had crossed that line, but I reckoned you just might have something to say about it. But Jimmy, that takes guts, and I like that. Yes, you can be sure, we're all proud of you."

Martin and his gran had much lost time to make up as they shared their news when he called on her that weekend. Martin summarised his whole sorry story, ending with, "And my time at 'Mick's Music' with Mick and Ralph could not have gone better. It settled me down, and helped me start saving seriously for a change."

As usual, Gran was unfazed. "I had a feeling, when I didn't hear from you, that maybe you had your reasons," she said calmly. "But, you know, you were always in my prayers. I did believe that things would work out for you.

There was only one answer to that. Martin looked his Gran in the eye, smiled and said simply, "Thanks, Gran. Thanks."

34

A Good Move

The following Monday, Graysfield headmaster Steve Smart called for an all-school assembly. He had plenty to say.

"The reports I have received from my staff regarding the St. Mary's football tournament have been of the highest measure, high praise indeed. Not only did Graysfield's two teams compete in the final, one of them actually received awards for outstanding sportsmanship – and that is something of the greatest importance. Because of this, and because this is an honour for our entire school, I consulted with the governors of the school at a meeting earlier today, and they have agreed that we should give the whole school an extra half-day's holiday to celebrate this honour. So, very well done, and thank you to both teams and their coaches – and a particular round of applause, please, for our fine Graysfield 'B' team, captained by Jimmy Evans. Jimmy, I recall you made an unconvincing start to your Graysfield career. But I can confidently say, you are turning things around now most impressively. Well done!"

Applause rang out in the hall as Jimmy and his team, as well as Graysfield 'A' and the two coaches, were given the praise they deserved.

"And now I have another announcement to make," the headmaster continued. "Over recent years, as I am sure everyone here is aware, Graysfield School has been going from strength to strength. An outstanding Ofsted report two years ago has been followed by record GCSE and A level results, as well as great success in music, drama and sport. No wonder Graysfield is a very popular school. Well now, the eagle-eyed of you will have noticed construction work fairly close to the school. Developers have obtained permission for up to seventy new houses and smaller dwellings to be built on that site. This, I am assured, is in no small way due to the success of our school, together with our widely publicised plans to build a new teaching block adjacent to the playing fields to allow us to offer even more subject choices for our GCSE and A level students. Many of you will know that houses near popular schools these days are like gold dust. So these homes will probably be snapped up quickly. If any of you have friends or contacts who just might wish to purchase a house near a friendly, successful secondary school, then I suggest you drop a word in their ears right away."

Martin, though not a full-time staff member, had been invited to attend the full school assembly, since he had so successfully led the Graysfield 'B' football team at St. Mary's. He already knew about the housing development, and had asked his gran whether she might consider downsizing and opting for a smaller house close to the school. "And if you want a paying lodger, I'm your man," he had added, reckoning the move could be good all round. He had been more than happy with his room above the music shop for two years, but probably now was the time to move into the next phase of his life.

Gran had considered the suggestion. "If I find something that suits me and also suits my bank balance," she said, "I'll certainly consider it."

True to her word, within a week she had visited the site office and put her name down for "a nice little house" close to Graysfield. Now she would be able to feel a part of the school and to enjoy visiting on many of their special occasions.

Everyone a winner!

35

LOOKING BACK

As Jimmy travelled home on the bus that Friday, he thought back to his early days at Graysfield. His nervousness and insecurity in the classroom. His anxiety over getting into the football team. His episodes with Kai, which had not exactly endeared him to the staff. His struggles to achieve anything worthwhile.

But now – wow, he felt different! Okay, those classroom lessons were still a bit of a struggle. But he did genuinely find some interest in most of them. Who could fail to connect with a history teacher who brought the subject to life as Mr. Kenny did? Or a head of art like Mr. Harris, who made painting so fascinating? Even the core subjects had their times of joy: drama in English, number puzzles during maths, experiments in science. On top of all that, he felt he had made his mark. It was hard to explain precisely, but he now felt so much more confident around the school. And for the headmaster himself to have said such encouraging words to him in assembly – "You are turning things around. ... Well done!" That was so encouraging; it really made him want to do well, not only for his own sake but for his school.

As Jimmy continued to ponder, it seemed there were certain characters who had given him the confidence, the courage, the motivation to turn things around. They were all people who perhaps knew what it was like to have to struggle, people who had not had it all their own way in their lives and careers.

There was Mr. Smith – tough as nails but always fair. He had been the one who had given Jimmy the challenge after he had 'messed up'. He hadn't closed the book on him, no – but he had said he wanted to see *"something extra"*. That had been a challenge Jimmy had been willing to accept. Smithy had also told the boys how he had had a tough upbringing, his parents having to work hard for every penny they earned. He had learnt the hard way, so seemed able to help those who had to work hard for success.

Martin too. Coaching the 'B' team, he had had a similar outlook to Smithy: you give your best, and with him it pays off. There was something, too, about the way in which he had offered to help at Graysfield, and how he clearly respected Smithy and his ways, that suggested to Jimmy that, for him too, life may have held a few unpleasant surprises.

Then there was Richard Adley, the man in the wheelchair, starting up his own academies and giving trophies for sportsmanship after his own setbacks. Here was another living example of someone Jimmy reckoned he could follow, a sort of hero or role model. No Ronaldo or Messi. But more reachable. Someone Jimmy reckoned might now make a difference in his life, just as his school coaches had already done in his short time at Graysfield.

He hopped off the bus and quickly walked home.

"Good day at school?" asked Mum, as he came in and flopped down at the kitchen table.

Jimmy poured himself a large glass of orange and took a long swig.

"Delicious!" replied Jimmy. "I mean, *really amazing*!"

He took another swig.

"Yes, Mum," he said emphatically. "*Really* good – and thanks for all your help." Then, after a little thought, he added "D'you know what, Mum? I reckon my 'red mist' days could be behind me."

Mum looked at Jimmy, paused a moment and then said, "Jimmy, I reckon you could be right."

Jimmy was remembering the advice she had shared with him what now seemed like ages ago: *"If you can hold yourself together, you'll become a better player also."*

"You certainly helped me sort things out," he said with feeling. "Thanks, Mum."

He glanced down at his half-open sports bag, and noticed one of his bright orange boots protruding from the top.

"Oh yes, and the boots!" he exclaimed. "They made a massive difference—" His voice tailed off, as if he were trying to express his thoughts. Then he added, "But, d'you know, Mum? I think I've been learning something. It's good to have talents, like in your legs and feet, but they seem to work even better if you use your head – you know, think cool. I reckon you've taught me that."

Jimmy drank some more orange, leaned back and closed his eyes. So much had happened. As he thought back, the words he remembered now were not from Smithy or Martin or Richard Adley – nor any adult. No, it was the voice of Ravi, cool and deliberate, that he recalled: *"Jimmy is always honest. He had to be true to himself. He had to do what he did."*

For a wild, brief moment Jimmy allowed himself to imagine what it might have been like had he chosen the alternative option. His team would have won the tournament, with him leading them to receive the winner's trophy – but at what cost? He would always have known that he had been less than truthful, and that he had denied his friend Kai of the winning goal and his schoolmates of their rightful victory and glory. He would have had to carry all that with him every day meeting up with those same schoolmates at Graysfield – and then beyond.

It did not bear thinking about. To use Ravi's words, he would not have been "true to himself". How grateful he was that something inside him at that moment had prevented him taking that sorry step.

Just then, the phone rang. Mum picked up the receiver. It was Smithy.

36

THE PHONE CALL

"Mrs. Evans, I'm sorry to trouble you," the head of games began, "I've got Richard Adley here. It was he who gave the awards at the St. Mary's football tournament. He would appreciate it if he could have a word with Jimmy, please. Of course, he needed to go through me first and then yourself before speaking to Jimmy. I can assure you this is genuine, and also, I believe, of interest to Jimmy."

Mum knew and trusted the games teacher, so she replied, "Sure, yes! He's right here. I'll put him on the line."

Turning to Jimmy, she said, "It's Mr. Smith. He's got Richard Adley there, wanting to speak to you."

Jimmy, intrigued, took the phone. "Hello?" he said, slightly nervously.

"Jimmy, hi! Richard Adley here," came the cheery reply. "I enjoyed meeting up with you and your team-mates on Saturday at St. Mary's. Jimmy, I'm setting up a footballing academy for players of your age, and I'm keen to find someone who can encourage the players on the field by example. These are players who've had it tough, and I need someone to lift them – someone who knows what it's like to be down, and who can help them try to rise through it. I asked several coaches individually, as well as contacting your headmaster, on Saturday; they all came up with the same suggestion: Jimmy Evans. So, would you like to give it some thought?"

Jimmy looked towards his mum.

"Mum, Mr. Adley's setting up an academy team, and he's asking if I would like to be in it..."

Mum considered for a moment before answering.

"If you want to do it, Jimmy, you accept – I won't stand in your way."

"Yes, please, Mr. Adley," he replied. "And thank you very much."

"Well, I am delighted at that," continued Mr. Adley, "and may I assume you would be happy to captain the team, and so lead them by your example?"

Jimmy again thought of those who had helped and guided him through his first year at Graysfield, particularly Smithy and Martin. He felt the joy of having been helped, and knew what a difference it had made to him. Richard Adley was now asking him to show the same kind of help and understanding to other players. Jimmy had no problem deciding on his answer.

"Yes, please. I would *love* to be captain," he replied enthusiastically. "Thank you for asking me!"

"That's great, Jimmy. Further details later. I'll be in touch."

Jimmy put the phone down. "Well, Mum, I reckon it doesn't get much better than that!"

"Jimmy, hi! Richard Adley here," came the cheery reply.

37

JUST THE BEGINNING

Just then, the door opened. It was Dad.

"Reg has arrived," he said. "He's taking over the shop to give me an early finish."

Mum fetched more glasses and a new bottle of orange juice from the fridge. She filled the glasses and gave one to Dad. "I think we can all celebrate! Your son has been chosen to captain Mr. Adley's football academy team," she announced cheerfully.

Dad was a man of few words – but when he did open his mouth, it was usually worth hearing. "He trusts you, Jimmy. He trusts you to do a job. And you will. I know you will." He raised his glass to Jimmy before downing the contents in record time. "Guess I needed that!" he joked.

Jimmy smiled. Those words from Dad – like those from his headmaster in the school assembly – meant so much to him. *It is great to know that people believe in you,* he thought. *Makes life good.*

"By the way," added Dad, "let me know when you play your next football match. I'll ask our friend Jenny to do the shop. Reg and I will come to check out those boots!"

"Aw, thanks, Dad!" replied Jimmy. "That'll be great!"

He finished his drink, leaned back in his chair and closed his eyes. *You won't please everyone,* he reasoned, as he sat thinking back over all that had happened recently, *but maybe if you're true to yourself, you can move on. Yes, moving on... And maybe this is just the beginning...* He paused for a moment. *I'll go with that,* he decided, triumphantly. *Yes-s-s!*

Mum and Dad smiled warmly at each other. They were proud of their son.

Jimmy drifted off to sleep.

A sound, satisfying sleep.

Dreaming of glorious goals...

And a pair of bright orange football boots.